The Face-off Phony

Look for other books in the Slapshots series.

The Face-off Phony

Gordon Korman

AN
APPLE
PAPERBACK

SCHOLASTIC INC.

New York Toronto London Auckland Sydney
Mexico City New Delhi Hong Kong

No part of this publication may be reproduced in whole or in part, or stored in
a retrieval system, or transmitted in any form or by any means, electronic,
mechanical, photocopying, recording, or otherwise, without written permission
of the publisher. For information regarding permission, write to Scholastic Inc.,
Attention: Permissions Department, 555 Broadway, New York, NY 10012.

ISBN 0-590-70629-2

12 11 10 9 8 7 6 5 4 3 2 1   0 1 2 3 4 5/0

Printed in the U.S.A.   40

First Scholastic printing, February 2000

For Crestview and Hillcrest,
where hockey began for me

░░░░░ _**Chapter 1**_

When things go bad for a hockey team, it's like the end of the world.

Think of the Mars Health Food Stars. They started off as the town joke. But they turned things around. I mean, after the All-Star tournament, they were one of the hottest teams in the Waterloo Slapshot League. And then they hit . . .

"_The Slump_," I dictated into my palm-size tape recorder, "by Clarence 'Chipmunk' Adelman, _Gazette_ sports reporter. I'm standing in the doorway of the Stars' locker room —"

"Out of my way, Chipmunk," grumbled Josh Colwin. He shoved past me and threw down his goalie mask in disgust. He took off his catching glove and glowered at the white rabbit's foot clutched in his fingers.

"You *stink*!" he accused the good-luck piece. "And because you stink, *I* stink!"

It was the second intermission of their game against the Ronny's Market Maple Leafs. The Leafs were dead last in the league standings. As a sports reporter, I knew this was the perfect chance for the Stars to snap their three-game losing streak. But after two pretty boring periods, the score was tied 1–1.

"We should be ahead by at least four goals," Trent Ruben complained. He was our assistant captain and the league's leading scorer. "What's wrong with me? I feel like I'm skating with bricks strapped to my feet!"

"Get away from that door!" shouted Brian Azevedo suddenly.

Mike Mozak froze in his tracks. "I have to go to the bathroom."

Brian was furious. "The last time we won, *Cal* went to the bathroom first after the second period! Are you trying to jinx us?"

Mike sat down. "Hurry up, Cal," he said irritably. "I really have to go."

"I'm busy," mumbled big Cal Torelli. From his duffel bag, he pulled out an enormous jar of pennies. He began to stick fistfuls of coins into the protector pockets of his hockey pants.

I stared at him. "What are you doing?"

"I need my lucky penny to start scoring again," Cal explained.

"How many lucky pennies do you have?"

"Just one," Cal replied. "But my mom threw it in the jar, and now I don't know which one it is. So I have to carry all of them, just in case."

"Well, I'm going to the bathroom!" Mike exclaimed defiantly.

"We're going to *lose*!" warned Brian.

Mike slumped back down. "Aw, come on!"

As painful as all this was, I left my tape recorder running. Face it: The reason a team falls apart is just as important as the reason it comes together and clicks. Someday, when I'm a reporter for *Sports Illustrated*, this could be the subject of a cover story. What makes a player who's a great skater on Wednesday forget how to stand on his feet by Saturday? What makes loyal teammates and good friends bicker and snap at one another like junkyard dogs? What makes sensible athletes decide that their very future depends on who goes to the bathroom, and in what order?

"I know how to change our luck," said Jared Enoch seriously. "Our fans have to do the wave."

Jared comes up with a lot of harebrained ideas, and the team is usually pretty understanding. But not today.

"The only wave around here is the tidal wave of stupidity that's coming out of everybody's mouths," said a quiet voice.

It was Alexia Colwin, Josh's twin sister. She was the Stars' captain, and the only girl in the Waterloo Slapshot League. She spoke so quietly that we could all tell how mad she was. Alexia operates on what I call reverse volume control. She gets quietest when everybody else would be yelling.

There was more. With Alexia, there was *always* more. "The next person who holds up a four-leaf clover is going to eat it." She was a no-nonsense kind of captain. "I don't mind losing as much as I can't stand these crazy superstitions. Cut it out. Mike — go to the bathroom before you explode."

Mike ran out just as Coach Boom Boom Bolitsky came in. Silence fell. If anyone knew about slumps, Boom Boom did. Our coach was a retired NHL player from the 1970s. I don't want to put him down or anything, but his whole career was kind of a slump. He was a last-round draft choice who got traded three times per season. That's when he wasn't getting sent down to the minors. If you look up *slump* in the dictionary, you'll probably find a picture of Boom Boom.

He would be easy to recognize. With his bulging eyes and skinny bent-over posture, he looked like a

4

six-foot praying mantis. He was completely bald in front, but he had a long frizzy ponytail in the back. Add to that a crooked nose and some missing teeth, and you've got the Stars' coach and sponsor.

But he was twice as nice as he was funny-looking. Boom Boom was the best. There was only one problem with having him for a coach. . . .

"Okay, don't panic," he soothed his players. "Slumps happen to everyone. Just don't change your whatchamacallit."

Your hairdo? Your underwear? Your mind? Your style of play?

"Those whosises shouldn't stand a thingamabob against a whatsit like us, with our experience and our dingus."

Get the picture? Our coach spoke a language all his own. When you know him for a while, you sort of learn how to translate some of it. For instance, I think he just said, "Those Leafs shouldn't stand a chance against a team like us, with our experience and our talent."

"You're right, Coach," said Trent, tossing aside his lucky skate tightener. "We'll get out of this slump by playing hard, not with any good-luck charm."

"The wave would really help, though," put in Jared.

Boom Boom looked startled. "The wave? Like in a big thingamajig stadium?"

Jared nodded enthusiastically. "Any team can win the Stanley Cup. But what's the one thing all the champions have in common? Their fans do the wave."

Poor Boom Boom. Dealing with Jared could be like pulling teeth. Coach Bolitsky was a retired hockey player. He didn't have that many teeth to spare.

"Well, Jared, uh —" He seemed really relieved when the buzzer sounded to call the teams for the third period.

]]]]] *Chapter 2*

There were a few catcalls mixed in with the cheers when the Stars stepped back on the ice. Some wise guy yelled, "Martians!" which really burned me up. You see, this was the Waterloo League, and all the players on our team went to school in Waterloo, but we didn't actually live in the city. Our town, Mars, was right across a narrow canal about two miles away. Trent was the only Waterloo kid on the Stars. The rest of us were Marsers — not Martians! — and this was our first year in the league. A lot of those Waterloo types thought it was better without us.

It took less than a minute of play, and there I was, dictating a new headline idea into my tape recorder: *"Slump Rages On."*

I'm not saying the Stars were playing like a

kindergarten team. In fact, one at a time, they looked fine. Trent was a great skater and stickhandler, and Alexia was the best checker in the league. Brian was a speedster, and Kyle Ickes skated backward better than most guys skate forward. He was so good at it that he actually kept a car mirror glued to his helmet. That way he could mount a whole backward rush and still see where he was going.

But they were somehow out of sync. It was like an orchestra of good musicians all playing the right notes, but at the wrong time.

Passes went wild; shots missed the net; line changes "on the fly" got bogged down, leaving one or two Stars to struggle against all five Maple Leafs. The power play was a big fizzle. They were awful.

With four minutes left to play, the Leafs scored to take a 2–1 lead. There was a gasp of horror from the Mars fans. They had watched their beloved Stars drop three in a row. But no one had dreamed they could possibly fall to the last-place Maple Leafs.

"Don't lose your heejazz!" bellowed Boom Boom. *Your cool.*

But the Stars couldn't even manage that. As the precious time ticked away, first Trent and, ten seconds later, Alexia, got called on penalties.

I looked at the clock in despair. One minute, thirty-seven seconds to play. If the Stars were going to stage a comeback, it would have to be a miracle. The rest of the game was a two-man power play for the Leafs! And the Stars' best players were both in the penalty box.

I looked from our two captains' red faces to see which three heroes Coach Bolitsky had sent out there to save the day. Jared — a winger — was at center. Cal and Brian were at his side. They seemed pretty outnumbered by all those blue shirts.

Oh, no! Jared lost the face-off! There was a scramble for the puck. And then something amazing happened — even by *Sports Illustrated* standards. A commotion beside me dragged my eyes away from the action. A scared, lost field mouse came running along the bleachers, causing havoc among the spectators. People screamed and leaped up on the bench to let it dart past.

"*Jared!*" came Boom Boom's foghorn. "Don't just stand there! *Skate!*"

I gawked. Instead of fighting for the puck, Jared was rooted to the ice, watching the disturbance that was rippling through the crowd. Of course, he couldn't spot the mouse. All he saw was people rising and sitting back down in a swaying movement that circled the rink. Just like —

"*The wave!!*" Jared bellowed in a fever of excitement. He sprang forward so fast that he took the puck away from the Leafs' center without even having to check the guy. Down the ice he sailed at top speed.

I admit it. I honestly read the name on the back of his jersey to make sure it was Jared. He was flying, riding what he thought was the wave. With the grace of Wayne Gretzky, he danced around one defender, beat the other with a lightning deke, and swooped down on the goalie.

"Shooooot!" howled Boom Boom.

And he did, a low slapshot that threaded the needle between the goalie's pads. Tie score, 2–2.

It was the first chance we'd had to celebrate for four long games, so the shouts and cheers were four times as loud as normal. Nail-biting time wasn't over, though. It was still a double power play for the Leafs. But remember — Ronny's Market had last place all sewn up. They squandered their opportunities, the clock ticked down, and we headed for sudden-death overtime.

In the five-minute extra period, Jared spent all his bench time screaming, "Do the wave again! The wave!"

But the spectators — who hadn't really done the wave to begin with — never got the message. By that time, the mouse was gone too.

The Stars picked up a little when Trent and Alexia got out of the penalty box. But every loose puck seemed to bounce the wrong way. They just couldn't get any offense going.

Finally, Kyle managed to chase down a rebound in the Stars' end. He whipped around and started on one of his famous reverse attacks. Kyle was hard to defend, since his whole body was always between you and the puck. But if you went around and tried to poke-check him, you were letting him past you. And he'd kill you with that great backward speed. Good teams had trouble handling him. For the last-place Leafs, he was a puzzle they would never solve.

Kyle passed off to Alexia, who went over the blue line with Trent at her side. In a trademark move, the two attackers crossed paths. Alexia flipped the puck to Trent, who one-timed a booming slapshot. The goalie made a stick save.

"Get the doojig!" yowled Boom Boom.

"The rebound!" I translated.

Both teams scrambled for the loose puck. Big Cal was our best digger. He was on that rebound two steps ahead of anybody else. But he tripped over Alexia's reaching stick. It was a spectacular spill — head over heels.

For a split second, he was upside down in the air. Out of his hockey pants spilled about twenty dollars worth of pennies.

Now, the last thing you want to drop on a hockey rink is a penny. It's warmer than the ice because it's been in your pocket. So the minute it hits, it sticks.

Instantly, the action in front of the net turned into a clown routine, as players from both teams tripped over two thousand tiny obstacles. And while the goalie was flat on his back, Trent popped the puck over him and into the net.

"Yee —"

I only got out a half cheer, because the referee was already waving his arms.

"No goal!" He pointed furiously at Cal. "Number sixteen just dropped a load of coins on the ice!"

"But it's my lucky penny!" Cal defended himself.

The referee stared. "*All* of them?"

"Calm down, Cal," called Boom Boom from the bench. "Pick up your thingamabobs, and let's finish this whatchamacallit."

But it wasn't as easy as that. Those thingamabobs were frozen into the ice. The referees had to scrape them up with shovels. After fifteen minutes of annoying delay, Cal got his penny collection back in a pail of slush.

"Oh, wow," Alexia commented sarcastically. "A copper Sno-Kone."

Cal found this so hilarious that he rolled along the bench, laughing into his bucket.

All this so we could play the last forty-nine seconds and wind up in a 2–2 tie.

Chapter 3 [[[[[

Man, did I ever need a jawbreaker!

When I'm depressed, it's the only thing that can help. That's how I got the nickname Chipmunk, you know. Ever since I was a little kid, I always had a great big ball of candy puffing out my cheek.

No more. Dental checkup. Eleven cavities. I hadn't had a jawbreaker in two months, three weeks, five days, fourteen hours, and thirty-two minutes — give or take a handful of miserable sugar-free seconds.

Not that even a Volcano-Hot Cinnamon Lava-Ball could erase the humiliation of what happened yesterday. I mean, the Stars had to try to celebrate barely squeaking out a tie against a last-place team! That's got to be harder than losing. The slump wasn't over. It was worse than ever.

It was driving me crazy. Less than two months ago, these same Stars beat the defending All-Star champions! A team where every player was the best of the best in his league! Back then it seemed like every rebound found its way onto a friendly stick, and even the goalposts were pulling for Mars Health Food. Now the Stars were skating like stumblebums. Team morale hit an all-time low.

And me? Well, a reporter is only as good as his story. I was writing about the Stars as a Cinderella team. But there's nothing in the fairy tale that talks about how Cinderella and the prince lived slumpily ever after.

That's why Monday morning found me at the school's old photocopy machine, printing up the latest issue of the Waterloo Elementary School *Gazette*. I had come up with the perfect story angle to jolt the Stars out of this killer funk.

I pulled a fresh copy out of the tray and flipped it over to the sports page.

STARS STILL ALIVE IN PLAYOFF RACE

by Clarence "Chipmunk" Adelman,
Gazette Sports Reporter

Even though the Stars are winless in their last four games, it's not yet over for the new team

from Mars. Believe it or not, if they can finish the regular season with three straight wins, they might still have a chance at the number-eight playoff spot, now held by the Flyers. . . .

"Clarence?" Mrs. Spiro poked her head in the door of the spare storeroom we used as the newspaper office. "What are you doing here? The bell's going to ring in five minutes."

"I'm just printing up the *Gazette*," I told her.

"I thought we were going to do that after school," she protested. "What's your hurry?"

"I want to get it out *today*," I replied. "It's really important for the Stars to read my latest article."

She rolled her eyes in that way she has. "Well, all right. But we have a very special English class in the art room. Don't be late."

"Gotcha, Mrs. Spiro."

Luckily, the machine was pretty fast. I ran off our usual hundred copies — plus a few extras. Mrs. Spiro can be really cheap about paper. Then I dropped a stack in the *Gazette* box in the office, another on the rack in the cafeteria, and slipped into the art room a millionth of a second before the bell.

"New *Gazettes*!" I barked, waving a handful of papers. "Hot off the press!" I began to move up and down the rows, handing out copies.

"Oh, great," sneered Happer Feldman, accepting his. "This'll come in handy. The bathroom's running low on toilet paper."

"Just what I needed," added Oliver Witt. He crumpled up the *Gazette* and blew his nose in it.

I said, "Hey, there's stuff in there about your team too!"

No sportswriter could ignore the Powerhouse Penguins, even though I would have loved to try. They were out in first place by a mile and sure to repeat as champions. They were even better last year when they had Trent.

"Wait a minute!" Happer stared at the headline in disgust. "Still alive in playoff race? The *Martians*?"

"*Really?*" Trent ran over and grabbed one of my papers. "Are you sure, Chipmunk? I thought we were out of it when we couldn't beat the Leafs."

"But the Flyers lost to the Oilers. See?" I showed him the league standings. "So we're still alive."

Oliver leaped to his feet. "The Oilers beat the Flyers? Impossible. The Oilers stink."

Happer snapped his fingers. "The Oilers have this new guy, Steve Stapleton." Happer's uncle was the league president, so Happer got a lot of inside info. He shot a mean look at Trent, his former line mate. "Watch out, Ruben. This kid must be good if he makes the Oilers into a winner. Don't count on being MVP again this year."

Alexia stuck her reverse volume control into the conversation. "I know you, Feldman," she said quietly. "You're scared of this guy Stapleton."

"Am not!"

I was upset. There was a new player — a *great* player — and nobody told the sports reporter? I stuck my hand in my pocket and switched on my tape recorder. "I've never heard of any Steve Stapleton. Does he go to the junior high?"

"He goes to County Junior High," Happer explained. "They let him on the Oilers after Kenny Gardner broke his leg."

"It figures," snorted Alexia. "The guy doesn't even live in town, and they beg him to join the Oilers. But it takes Mars thirty years to get a team in this crummy league."

Trent shrugged. "There are a lot of farms east of the city. They have Waterloo addresses, but their kids all go to County. He probably lives over there."

"At least he's from Earth," added Oliver nastily.

Another dig at us Marsers. You can't imagine the space alien jokes we put up with.

Mrs. Spiro breezed in, so we hustled back to our seats.

"Good morning, everyone," she greeted us with a smile. "You're probably wondering why we're meeting in the art room. Well, this is the day that the whole sixth grade becomes parents. You are here to prepare your egg babies."

The groan that rose from every throat rattled the windows. Oh, no! Not egg babies! She did this to the grade sixes's last year, and they all agreed it was the biggest pain in the butt that ever happened to them. Now it was our turn.

It all starts with a hollowed-out eggshell. It's your job to paint it, name it, and pretend it's a real baby. You have to keep it safe; you can't leave it alone; if you go somewhere, you have to pay a baby-sitter. I'm not making this up! And the craziest part is that this waste of time goes on for two weeks!

"Furthermore," Mrs. Spiro continued, "you'll each be required to keep an hour-by-hour journal. You'll need to list the location of your egg baby and the name of the caregiver." She smiled sweetly. "Don't think you're going to get your mothers to take over the whole job. You can't be away from your egg baby for more than three hours a day."

She turned serious. "There are some lessons that can't be measured with A's, B's, and C's. This experiment will teach you the responsibility of being a parent. I consider it the most important project of your grade-six year. Don't even think about making a joke out of it."

Then each of us was given an egg. The first order of business was to hollow it out.

We had step-by-step instructions. You make a pin-hole in each end. Then you blow in one hole until all that yolky stuff comes out the other. Simple.

Mine broke. I guess I'm a hard blower. So while everyone else was painting faces on their egg babies, I was starting on another egg.

That one broke too.

Mrs. Spiro glowered at me as she handed over egg number three. "Clarence, this is a baby! You have to be gentle."

"It's not born yet until all the yolk's out," I defended myself.

I started over. Everyone else was now gluing cotton balls into shoe boxes to create a "safe environment" for their egg babies. I was the last one done. When I heard the bell for period two, I painted on a quick face. It looked pretty bummed out. I'm sure I looked even worse.

I ran for the door.

"Not so fast," Mrs. Spiro ordered. "Your egg baby is a person. He or she has to have a name."

I peered into my shoe box. Anything halfway

round always reminds me of jawbreakers. The white ones are called Cool Minty Icebergs.

"His name is Minty," I announced.

Looking at me suspiciously, she recorded it in her book.

At three-thirty, the school halls were impossible. Every sixth-grader was hugging a big shoe box and walking slowly and carefully. Major traffic jam.

The buzz of conversation was all about baby names: Ashley, Jonathan, lots of Leos, after Leonardo DiCaprio, the actor. Alexia named hers Amelia (Amelia Earhart, the legendary pilot); most of the Stars chose famous hockey names: Wayne, Mario, Gordie, Eric, Dominic — you get the picture. Players from the other teams picked the same kind of stuff. Mine was the only Minty.

So there we were with our shoe boxes, trying to make our way out to our bus. The Waterloo kids called it *Pathfinder* after the NASA Mars mission. Cracking on the Marsers as usual.

I knew something was up when I saw the crowd of giggling wise guys at our bus stop. They parted to reveal a big sign:

FIRST NATIONAL BANK OF MARS

Beside it was a large washtub that somebody had filled with dirty snow. A smaller sign, MARTIAN LIFE SAVINGS, had an arrow pointing to a handful of pennies in the slush. A shovel labeled WITHDRAWALS was jammed into the center.

I was so mad. Leave it to those Waterloo jerks to take Cal's accident with the pennies and turn it against all of Mars. I set down my shoe box and snatched up that stupid NATIONAL BANK sign to tear it into pieces.

"Oh, don't rip it!" protested Cal. "I want to add it to my joke collection!"

"But it's a joke on *you*!" Alexia whispered furiously.

"But it's so funny!" guffawed Cal. Our winger could get hysterical reading the telephone book.

The bus pulled up, and the Waterloo crowd laughed even harder. I turned around and found out why. The right front tire had driven directly over my shoe box. It was as flat as a tortilla.

"Uh-oh," said Jared. "I hope your egg baby didn't break."

Like an empty eggshell has a fighting chance against a twenty-ton bus.

I picked up the squashed box and looked inside what was left of the lid. Minty was powder.

▌▌▌▌▌ _Chapter 4_

My _Gazette_ headline did the trick. The Stars were blown away that they still had a slim chance of making the playoffs. It injected hope into their veins. Hope and purpose. The team voted to hold extra practices to break out of this slump.

The problem was that we weren't scheduled for ice time at the community center until Thursday. There was an outdoor rink in Mars, but it wasn't very good during warmer weather. The Stars showed up for practice the next afternoon to find the ice surface was soup.

"Oh, man," complained Josh. "We should have brought our bathing suits."

"That's a good one!" roared Cal. "I get it — because the rink is all water!"

"But how are we going to practice?" asked Brian.

At that moment, the Mars Health Food truck rattled up, and there was Boom Boom.

"Hop in the back," he invited. "I've rented gizmos."

Gizmos turned out to be Rollerblades. So the team practice took place on the health food store's concrete parking lot.

The coach's wife volunteered to act as the caregiver for everybody's egg babies. Remember, we weren't allowed to let those dumb things out of our sight unless we had a sitter.

I decided to hand over my shoe box along with the others. Yes, I had a new egg baby, starting from scratch with the pinpricks and the blowing — the whole whoop.

Mrs. Bolitsky frowned at the name on my shoe box. "Grape-O?"

Mrs. Spiro had suggested that I paint this egg baby, just to give it more character. The only open color was purple — just like Grape-ola Mega-Bombs, jawbreakers with real fruit juice explosions inside.

I would have loved to explain this to Mrs. Bolitsky. But I have trouble speaking when she's around. All the guys do. She is so beautiful, so breathtaking, so unbelievably gorgeous — forget it. You can't use words to describe Mrs. B. I mean, she'd been looking kind of tired lately, and maybe a little pale. She was probably worried about the team's slump. But she was still a thousand times prettier than the most amazing supermodel.

With Grape-O in her capable hands, I was free to report on the practice. It wasn't exactly Stanley Cup play. The driveway was sloped and had big potholes, and nobody knew how to stop on Rollerblades. There were collisions galore as the Stars went careening over ruts, curbstones, rocks, and twigs, chasing after the ball — yes, I said ball. You can't use a puck on pavement.

So there wasn't much real hockey going on. But I noticed something that was just as important — maybe more. For the first time in a month, the Stars were having fun. They were laughing and cheering, teasing one another, and showing off. Cal took wild slicing slapshots that sent the ball straight up. Trent was mixing hockey with soccer, making passes with his helmeted head. Jared had abandoned his stick and was circling the parking lot, doing a one-man wave, complete with crowd sound effects. Even no-nonsense Alexia was trying out some of her old spins and jumps from figure skating, stick and all.

Boom Boom was impressed. "Hey, where'd you

learn that thingamajig?" He tried to copy her toe loop and ended up flat on his back on the pavement.

"Boom Boom, are you all right?" Mrs. B. came running out to see to her husband.

"Our egg babies!" We stampeded into the store to watch our shoe boxes.

Since the guys were tongue-tied around Mrs. B., Alexia explained the situation to the Bolitskys: Even if the coach had split his head open like a watermelon, and his blood was draining down the sewer, the baby-sitter may not abandon her duties long enough to dial 911. In Spiro Land, that makes sense.

Luckily, Boom Boom was okay. He even helped serve the after-practice doojig — *snack* — tofu tamales. We all followed the secret Stars' rule: No one is allowed to tell the Bolitskys how awful their health food is.

"Coach," said Trent, looking a little ashamed. "I guess we didn't get in a whole lot of practice out there today. Sorry for all the fooling around."

Boom Boom was surprised. "That dingus was just what we needed — to blow off a little whatsit. Next heejazz, you play to have fun, and I guarantee we'll be racking up the thingamabobs."

"Wins," translated the coach's wife.

"And that means the playoffs, right, Chipmunk?" prompted Josh.

"It's kind of complicated," I admitted. "We have to win our games, and the Flyers have to lose at least two. But not the one against the Mighty Ducks. That would put the Ducks ahead of us in the tie-breaking formula." I frowned. "And a bunch of other stuff has to happen too."

"But it's possible," Brian persisted.

The coach nodded. "But don't get your doojigs up."

"Your hopes," translated his wife.

Alexia took out a dollar and handed it to Mrs. B.

The coach's wife looked shocked. "What's this for?"

"Baby-sitting," Alexia explained. "A dollar an hour. That's the egg-baby rate."

Mrs. Bolitsky's jaw dropped when she saw that we were all digging out money for her. "Oh, no," she laughed. "I couldn't possibly accept that."

"But you have to," said Trent. "And we each need a receipt to prove that we paid."

Boom Boom was thunderstruck. "But they're not babies! They're just empty doohickeys!"

"*You* know that," I sighed. "And *we* know that. But just try to tell it to Mrs. Spiro."

Chapter 5 ⎣⎣⎣⎣⎣

Saturday's game was the first chance for the Stars to prove that the slump was really over. The team looked loose and confident. But our opponents were the Ferguson Ford Flames, and they had already clinched a playoff spot — fifth place overall. Not exactly the Penguins, but a solid contender. They weren't going to be easy to beat.

Coach Bolitsky's pep talk was pretty low-key. Then he clapped his hands and said, "Let's get out there on the whatsit!"

We all stared at him.

Finally, Trent spoke up. "But, Coach, where's your wife?"

"Oh, she's not feeling well today," Boom Boom replied. "She has a thingamadingus."

Don't quote me, but I think that's a headache.

"But —" Josh persisted. "But that means we have no baby-sitter."

Boom Boom looked at the shoe boxes clutched in our hands. Except for Mike, who was in grade seven, every single Star had one, including the team reporter — me.

"Nobody's going to steal them," the coach reasoned. "Leave them here in the whatchamacallit."

"Not without a sitter," Alexia replied. "I know it sounds crazy, but those are the rules."

When Boom Boom is deep in thought, the praying-mantis eyes whirl in his head. When they stopped spinning, they were focused on me. "Give them to Chipmunk."

"Oh, no, " I said seriously. "I can't report on the game if I have to juggle eleven shoe boxes."

So we took a big shopping bag, padded it with some towels, and placed the egg babies lovingly inside.

Jared looked worried. "Are you sure Chipmunk's responsible enough to be a caregiver? His last egg baby got run over by a bus, you know."

"That wasn't my fault," I mumbled. "It was a tragic accident."

Alexia gave me the bag. "This doesn't leave your

arms," she ordered. "Don't set it down on the floor where it can get stepped on."

"But I need my hands free for my tape recorder," I protested. "I'm a working reporter."

Her voice dropped to nothing. "You're a dead man if I have to blow the goo out of another egg." She took the handles and slipped them over my head so the bag hung around my neck.

As I followed the team out, I caught a glimpse of myself in the mirror. My mom has an old picture of me in a sailor suit. It's the only time I ever looked stupider than right then.

The bleachers were already filling up, so I had to hurry to get my usual spot behind the Mars Health Food bench. A lot of Marsers always come to support the Stars, not just parents and brothers and sisters of the players. After being kept out of the league for so long, our little town felt that having a team was a pretty big deal.

I sat next to Mr. Gunhold, who was sort of an old friend of mine. He owned Toute Sweet, the best candy store in Mars. Some of the happiest moments of my life were in his shop, deciding which jawbreaker was going to spend the next two hours tucked into my cheek. That was pre-dentist, of course.

"Hi, Mr. Gunhold. How's business?"

"Not bad." He shrugged. "Considering I lost my best customer."

Mr. Gunhold had the biggest stomach I've ever seen. Personally, I suspect he's his own best customer.

"Come on, boys!" he cheered in a voice that came right from the gut.

At the blue line, Alexia shot him a look that scorched clear through her visor.

"And girl!" he added quickly.

The Stars were testing Josh with some practice breakaways when Cal suddenly stopped short in a shower of snow.

"What's wrong?" asked Josh.

"Look!" Cal pointed down. There, just outside the goal crease, was a shiny penny. He reached down to pick it up. It was frozen under the glassy surface of the rink.

Brian skated over. "You think it's one of yours?"

"It looks kind of familiar," Cal admitted.

Alexia was totally disgusted. "Well, gee," she said sarcastically. "It's round and it says 'one cent.' That's a dead giveaway."

Josh bent over to examine the coin. "I guess the refs missed it last week. And after the Zamboni went over it a few times, it got permanently frozen into the ice."

"Wouldn't it be funny if it turned out to be the lucky one?" put in Kyle.

Cal looked hopeful. "Do you think it's possible? None of the ones they scraped up caught my eye."

Alexia groaned. "Haven't we just been through all this?"

Brian dug at the trapped penny with the toe of his skate. "At least you don't have to worry about bringing it to the rink," he said to Cal. "It's here for good."

From the opening face-off, I could tell that the Flames were no pushovers. They didn't have a superstar like Trent, but they had solid skaters at every position. And one kid, a defenseman named Rusty Kay, was the best passer I've ever seen.

When he lugged the puck out of his own end, you could tell that he knew where every single teammate was. At exactly the right moment, he'd find one of the forwards with a feed that was so delicate and perfect that it flew like a homing pigeon onto the guy's stick. His brilliant setups created two-on-ones and great scoring chances. Josh had to be sharp to keep the Stars from falling behind in the first few minutes.

Then Rusty hit his left winger with a beautiful pass that would have been a clean breakaway. Brian had no choice but to trip the kid at center ice. Up shot the referee's arm, and the Flames went on the power play.

Trent and Alexia were both great penalty killers. But when Rusty Kay stationed himself at the blue line to direct a power play, he was almost like a basketball point guard running a half-court offense.

Alexia came out of the "box" to challenge him. It was a gutsy move, but a big mistake. Rusty feathered a pass right between her skates. It was perfectly aimed for the center to one-time a slapshot past Josh. 1–0, Flames.

"*No-o-o-o!*" howled Mr. Gunhold. I never knew he was such a fan.

"This is the key moment for the Stars," I murmured into my tape recorder. "Will the slump continue? Or can they shrug off this goal and fight back?"

Beside me, Mr. Gunhold bellowed, "*Go-o-o-o!*"

My sound-level needle went off the scale.

I looked up to see Trent with the puck. I guess he decided to show that he didn't take a backseat to any player in this league. He was stickhandling so fast that the taped blade was just a blur. The deke he put on Rusty had the kid falling in two directions at the same time. He cruised in on goal, faked a wrist shot, then pulled the puck to his backhand, and slid it into the open corner. It was a Ruben Special.

"The slump is over!" I roared into my tape recorder as we rose to our feet, cheering.

I doubt I was loud enough to be heard over Mr. Gunhold's ecstatic yelling beside me.

"Do the wave! Do the wave!" Jared exhorted the crowd.

Nobody paid any attention to him.

Coach Bolitsky left his skaters on the ice. But the Flames changed lines. On came Moose McCoy, who centered their second unit.

Trent took his spot in the face-off circle opposite Moose. But the big seventh-grader was more interested in Alexia.

"Hey, missy. I hear you think you can bodycheck."

"If you touch her," growled Trent, "it better be a legal hit."

I could see what was coming. Alexia wasn't troubled by bullies like Moose. What she couldn't stand was having somebody else fight her battles.

"Butt out, Ruben," she snarled.

"But Lex —"

"I can take care of myself!" Her reverse volume control was cranked down to practically zero.

I smelled trouble. Moose was a burly junior high kid with a bad attitude. After the face-off, the play stayed in the neutral zone. Alexia picked up the puck near the red line. Even from the bleachers, I could see Moose targeting her.

"Look out!" warned Trent.

But it was too late. Moose took two monumental strides and hammered her into the glass. She crumpled to the ice, winded and gasping.

Chapter 6 \\\\\\

Boom Boom vaulted over the boards even before the referee blew his whistle. "Injured whosis!"

"I'm not injured!" Alexia wheezed, trying to struggle to her feet.

"Stay down!" ordered Trent.

Well, that would have brought Alexia upright even if someone had parked a car on top of her. When it came to pure toughness, no one was a match for the only girl in the Waterloo Slapshot League.

Boom Boom watched her in concern. "Need help getting to the dingus?"

"I'm not going to the dingus." Alexia stuck her jaw out at Moose. "I have some unfinished business here on the ice."

But the coach was no dummy. He got Alexia and

her line over to the bench and sent the second unit out to face Moose and Company.

It's pretty easy to dismiss Boom Boom as an airhead because of the way he looks and all that thingamajig talk. But he's a really sharp guy. For the rest of the period, he managed to work the line changes so that Alexia Colwin and Moose McCoy never shared the same ice.

"What's the matter, missy?" Moose called every time he passed by the Stars' bench. "You chicken?"

And Alexia smoldered like a wet campfire.

After the first intermission, the Flames came out strong. Rusty picked up his second and then his third assist as his team went ahead 3–1.

I thought Mr. Gunhold was going to yell the building down. The only peace and quiet I got was when his mouth was occupied with a supertanker of popcorn. He offered me some, but I didn't want to get any of the hot butter on the egg babies. Who could tell what kind of a crime that would be in Mrs. Spiro's eyes?

The Stars' offense bogged down. For a few minutes, I was afraid they were slipping back into their slumpy ways. Especially when Moose took a penalty, and the Stars' power play couldn't manage a single shot on goal.

Then, just before the end of the period, Mike fired one of his famous shovel shots through heavy traffic and into the Flames' net. 3–2, Ferguson Ford.

During the second intermission, the coach was excited. "This is it!" he crowed, his long shaggy ponytail bouncing behind his hairless crown. "We've hung close all game! Now it's time to do whatsit!"

"The wave?" asked Jared hopefully.

"*Win!*" exclaimed Boom Boom. "We're in striking distance. It's time to put them away."

Alexia was really antsy. "Coach, you've got to put me out there against that guy Moose!"

He just plain ignored her. "We're the better hee-jazz today," he told the team. "The difference is that whosis Rusty. We've got to find a way to mess up his passing."

But that was easier said than done. In the third period, Rusty continued to thread the needle to his forwards.

"He's unbeatable!" panted Cal. "If you attack him, he slides one right through your legs!"

"But if you hang back," added Kyle, his rearview mirror foggy from huffing and puffing, "you're giving him all the time in the world to find someone with a clear path to the net!"

The shots-on-goal counter read 24–9 in favor of the Flames.

Then — totally by accident — Brian solved the mystery of Rusty Kay. Brian was the fastest Star, but he couldn't skate backward to save his life. With Rusty coming at him, he had no choice but to try to reverse.

"*No-o-o-o!*" chorused the entire Stars' bench. Kyle went backward, and Brian went forward. They were the perfect defense pair — except when they tried to switch specialties.

Brian lost his balance just as Rusty made his pass. But as Brian flopped on the ice, his stick flailed out beside him.

Clink!

The puck knocked into it and rolled harmlessly out past the blue line. It was Rusty's first pass all day that had missed its target.

I thought Boom Boom was going to go through the roof. He vaulted up on the bench, bellowing, "That's it!"

"That's *what*?" cried Mr. Gunhold, raining popcorn all over my egg babies.

But Trent understood perfectly. The next time Rusty lined up a pass, Trent dropped to one knee in front of him, placing the shaft of his stick flat along the ice. The puck caromed off the butt end, and Trent pounced on it in a split second. Rusty skated after him, but this was Trent Ruben. He was gone.

Powered by the cheers of the Mars fans, he flew past the red line, swooped over the blue line, and fired a graceful rising wrist shot that beat the goalie just over his blocker.

Tie game, 3–3.

From then on, both teams shifted into overdrive. I put a new headline idea on tape: *"Barn-burner!"* because the action never stopped. It never even slowed down.

I thought the Stars might have a slight edge; a loss or even a tie in this game would finish our playoff chances. But there was a disadvantage too: Boom Boom was still keeping Alexia away from Moose. That meant he couldn't double-shift his best winger.

"Last minute of play in the game," came the P.A. announcement.

It was desperation time. Coach Bolitsky did what he'd been avoiding all game: He sent Alexia over the boards when Moose was on the ice.

"Don't do whatchamacallit!" he ordered sternly.

She grinned at him. "I promise, Coach." And as she skated away, I distinctly heard her mumble, "Because I'll be too busy doing thingamabob."

The face-off was in the Flames' end, to the left of their goalie. The referee held the puck over the sticks of Trent and Moose, the two centers. Suddenly, Trent jumped the gun and slapped at the dot.

"Hey, hey, hey," said the referee. "Not yet."

I was surprised. Trent was the quickest face-off man in the league. He didn't need to guess at the drop. He was fast enough to wait for it.

But it happened again. He slapped at Moose's stick, and the referee blew his whistle. The official had no choice but to wave Trent out of the circle.

All at once, I understood. Trent hadn't disqualified himself by mistake. He'd done it on purpose. He was giving Alexia a chance to face-off against Moose.

Alexia's chin was stuck out so far that it arrived at the dot before she did.

"Back for more?" the big jerk grinned.

Face-off! The referee made the drop and jumped out of the way.

Moose went for the puck, but Alexia went straight for Moose.

Crunch! She rammed her shoulder up into his chest. But Moose was so big that he didn't fall. Instead, he began to glide backward, the puck caught in the crook of his stick. Alexia dug her skates into the ice and shoved with all her might, and Moose picked up speed. The seventh-grader struggled to free himself, but Alexia had too much momentum. Smiling into his astonished face, she pushed him clear out of the face-off circle, past the net, and —

Wump!

Moose hit the boards and dropped to the ice, dazed. He had just managed to haul himself upright when both teams went in after the loose puck.

Crash!

He was slammed back against the boards again.

"Double whammy!" I cheered into my tape recorder.

Alexia dug out the puck and centered it to Jared. But his wrist shot bounced harmlessly off the goalie's pad.

"Rebound!" bellowed Mr. Gunhold beside me. His face was as red as a tomato.

But at this point, he was no louder than the rest of the Mars fans. *These* were the Stars we knew and loved — a swarming, hard-checking offense! It was the best they'd played for a whole month! I glanced up at the clock. Only twenty seconds to go!

The Flames' goalie dove on the rebound, but Trent poked it loose with his stick. Rusty got to it first and hacked a clearing pass. But Kyle reversed out of nowhere and blocked it with his body before it could cross the blue line.

"Shoooot!!" bellowed Boom Boom, Mr. Gunhold, me, and about a hundred other people.

With five seconds to go, Kyle unloaded a blistering slapshot from the point.

"Wide!" I gasped in horror. The blast was going to miss by at least a foot.

Suddenly, Alexia muscled free of her checker and stuck her stick into the path of the speeding puck. It hit the tip and deflected past the goalie and into the net. Final score: 4–3, Stars.

The community center rocked as the Mars fans roared to their feet.

"Picture-Perfect Tip-in!" I shrieked out my headline idea in the midst of the celebration.

The Stars' bench cleared. Mr. Gunhold hurled the rest of his popcorn straight up in the air. Then he turned his giant stomach to me and enfolded me in a mammoth bear hug.

Cra-a-a-a-ack!!

Uh-oh. Humpty Dumpty.

What a coward! I didn't have the guts to check inside the shopping bag. I waited until I had the whole team gathered around me in the locker room before even opening it.

"How bad is it?" I was still looking away.

The chorus of groans provided my answer. I risked a downward glance. Dust.

"Hey," said Boom Boom. "Who busted your doohickeys?"

"The team reporter," seethed Alexia.

"It wasn't my fault," I defended myself. "Blame Mr. Gunhold."

"Wait a minute." Trent reached into the bag and dug around the eggshell crumbs. He came up with a single unbroken egg baby. It was bright green, with sunglasses and a goatee painted on its smiling face.

"*Wendell!!*" Jared cried joyously. He snatched the egg baby from Trent and stroked it with his hockey glove. "I thought you were a goner, pal!"

"Thanks a lot, Chipmunk!" Kyle snarled sarcastically.

"Yeah, way to go, Einstein!" added Josh.

"As a baby-sitter, you should stick with being a reporter," put in Brian.

"Aw, come on, guys," I wheedled. "Mine got crushed, too, you know."

"But yours *always* die," Cal reminded me. "It's a new experience for us."

"Enough of this negative thingamabob," announced Boom Boom sharply. "I'll be waiting for you at the doojig." He set out for the delivery van, which acted as the team bus on game days.

Trent lived in Waterloo near the community center, so he was the only walker. He threw his duffel bag over his shoulder. "Great game, everybody. See you Monday."

He was almost out the door when Alexia stopped him. "Not so fast, hotshot."

I could see the problem right away. By setting her up to face-off against Moose, Trent had done Alexia a *favor*. Our captain could be weird about stuff like that.

Trent dropped his bag with a groan. "All right, I confess. I got thrown out of the face-off circle on purpose. I wanted you to have a chance to get even with Moose. I'm sorry. It'll never happen again."

She rolled her eyes. "Cut it out, Ruben. I just wanted to say thanks." And she picked up her own duffel and walked out.

Stunned, Trent turned to Josh. "Am I crazy, or did I *finally* do the right thing with your sister?"

Josh shrugged. "I've lived with Lex for twelve years. Trust me — there *is* no right thing."

Chapter 7 \\\\\

Mrs. Spiro was not pleased when she found out about our egg babies. The whole team, except for Jared, had to stay after school in — you guessed it — the art room. While we were blowing yolk into paper towels, Mrs. Spiro gave us a lecture about "taking this project a little more seriously."

Personally, I don't believe real babies are as delicate as eggshells. If they were, very few of us would live to grow up. Mrs. Spiro probably never thought of that.

The weekend hockey results were on everyone's lips. The big news was that the Oilers won again. They destroyed the Panthers 6–0 yesterday — a huge upset. The new kid, Steve Stapleton, scored four goals and assisted on the other two.

Alexia painted the finishing touches of a space helmet on her new egg baby, Sally (named after Sally Ride, the astronaut). She shot Trent a dazzling smile. "Could there be a new hotshot in town?" She loved razzing Trent.

Her assistant captain wasn't taking the bait. "Guys like Steve Stapleton get people interested in junior hockey," he said seriously. "He'll be good for the league — you know, if he's as talented as everybody thinks."

"He won't be good for the goalies," put in Josh, placing Dominic II in his shoe box. "What if he scores fifty on me?"

"We're going to find out," his sister told him. "We play the Oilers in the last game on the schedule."

That wasn't soon enough for me. No way could the *Gazette* sports reporter wait until the end of the season to get a look at the biggest news story in the league.

That's why I was rushing to get this egg degunked. The Oilers were practicing at the community center right now. It was the perfect chance for me to watch Steve Stapleton play, and maybe even interview him afterward.

"Don't blow so hard, Clarence," Mrs. Spiro admonished me. "You don't want to hurt her."

"Her?" I repeated.

"Maybe you'd be a little more careful if you had a baby girl to look after," she suggested.

"Great idea, Mrs. Spiro." (Dumb idea, Mrs. Spiro.)

I reached for the pink paint — you know, more feminine and all that. The face got kind of smudged. Either that or my "daughter" had two noses. Hey, I was in a hurry!

Mrs. Spiro sighed. "All right, Clarence. What's her name?"

Well, how could I look at something round and pink without dreaming of Ultra Quarks, the most delicious jawbreakers ever invented? They taste like a real peanut butter and jelly sandwich!

"Her name is Quark," I told her.

"Quark?" she repeated. "She's a little girl! What kind of a name is Quark?"

But I was already running down the hall, the shoe box tucked in the crook of my arm like a football.

I made it to the community center in time to catch the last ten minutes of the Oilers' workout. "Stapleton practice, March seventh," I dictated into my tape recorder. "Steve is number —"

It took about a millionth of a second to spot him. Number twelve. He wasn't bigger than the rest of the guys. In fact, he was kind of skinny. But he definitely had *something*. Call it perfect hockey balance.

Knees bent, low to the ice — just what you see when you watch the NHL stars. I mean, the whole team was checking him, but they couldn't knock him off the puck.

"He moves like his skates are part of his feet," I recorded.

I watched him fake out five guys and score. His shot was a bullet — accurate and deadly. It was harder than Trent's shot, and the release was quicker. As much as I hated to admit it, Steve was just plain better than Trent in every way.

Man, was this news! It was an even bigger story than when Trent got kicked off the Penguins and sent over to the Stars.

I skulked around outside the locker room after the practice, brainstorming questions to ask Steve. Hockey stuff — you know, about his style, and what NHL players he admired.

The door opened, and Ned Gallagher, the Oilers' captain, stepped out. He took one look at my shoe box and snorted a laugh at me. "Quark? Hey, Chipmunk — is it your egg baby or your science project?"

Ned was a good guy — sort of a class-clown type. He was in grade seven, so he was done with the egg-baby part of life, lucky him.

"Is Steve Stapleton coming out soon?" I asked.

He looked suspicious. "Why?"

I shrugged. "I have to interview him."

"Oh, don't bother Steve," Ned said airily. "I can tell you everything you need to know."

"Well, I suppose we could start that way," I offered reluctantly. I clicked on my tape recorder. "How long has he been playing hockey?"

"Forever," Ned replied. "A really long time. Not *that* long," he interrupted himself. "Just — long."

You know how Spider-Man has spider sense? Well, I have the same kind of thing — not spider, obviously, but a sixth sense for reporters. Whenever there's a news story hiding somewhere, my reporter's sense tingles. Right now it was zapping me like a dentist's drill with no novocaine.

When the other Oilers began to emerge, every single one of them had something to add to my interview. Pretty soon there were seven or eight guys out there telling me who Steve's favorite player was.

"Mark Messier."

"Jaromir Jagr."

"Wayne Gretzky."

"Joe Sakic."

Four Oilers gave me four names.

I frowned. "Well, which one is it?"

They started again. This time they listed four *different* players.

"Why don't we ask Steve himself?" I suggested. "He should be coming out any minute."

And they all started babbling about how Steve can't be disturbed. Why? Was he performing open-heart surgery?

I clicked off the recorder. "I'm going to wait for Steve."

Eventually, they left me alone. But they hung around the snack bar. I could tell they were watching me.

Sometimes you have to be really patient to be a reporter. It took *twenty minutes* for Steve to emerge.

He had blond hair and fair skin. His eyes were light brown and *very* sharp. I hadn't even opened my mouth, and already he was giving me the feeling that I was wasting his valuable time.

I hit record. "Hey, Steve, how about answering a few questions for the *Gazette*?"

The sharp eyes narrowed. "For the what?" He was a fast talker for a farm kid. He reminded me of one of those New York City police officers on TV.

"The Waterloo Elementary School *Gazette*," I explained. "I'm the sports reporter, Chipmunk Adelman."

"What kind of a name is Chipmunk?"

I flashed him my chipmunk face, making the ball in my cheek with my tongue. "I used to have a jaw-breaker problem."

"Well, I have an interview problem," he informed me. "I'm a really shy guy, okay? Nothing personal." And he turned his slender back on me and walked away.

Some athletes have a stormy relationship with the press.

I watched him wade into the crowd of high-fiving teammates at the snack bar. He was laughing and slapping right along with them. Shy, eh? He looked about as shy as a tiger shark.

"He's hiding something," I whispered into my tape recorder.

Cautiously, I edged over. The Oilers were fighting over who was going to get to buy Steve a hot chocolate. I looked at the pile of sports bags at their feet. Steve's was the red one. Now, I'm not a snoop, but when you're a reporter, you train yourself to notice stuff. Things a detective might pick up — details, clues, *unzipped red duffel bags*!

Tucking my shoe box under my arm, I pushed through the crowd up to Steve. When he turned his head, I dropped to the floor and set Quark down behind me. Pretending to tie my shoe with one hand, I rifled through his duffel with the other.

"You again?!" Rough hands grabbed me by the collar. I was yanked to my feet, where I came face-to-angry-face with Steve Stapleton. For not such a big guy, he was as strong as a bull.

"Kid," he snarled in my face, "when I say no interviews, I mean no interviews!"

"But —" I protested.

He shoved me. "Get out of here!"

I went flying. As I staggered back, I stepped on my shoe box. My foot broke right through the lid.

Crack!

"Oh, no!" I peeked inside. Being a girl hadn't helped Quark. She was in about twenty pink pieces.

But my heart was soaring. Another busted eggshell was a small price to pay for solving the riddle of the mysterious Steve Stapleton.

Chapter 8 \{\{\{\{\{

On Tuesday, the temperature suddenly dropped thirty degrees, so the Stars held their next practice after school at the outdoor rink in Mars. Wouldn't you know it? I had to stay in detention to hollow out another egg baby, Guava (named after Guava-berry Mouth Manglers). Today of all days — when I had the sports scoop of the century to tell every-body!

It took forever. I missed the school bus and had to wait around for the Waterloo Transit to get me back to Mars. I sprinted all the way from the bus stop. By the time I got to the rink I was huffing and puffing so badly that the players thought I was having a heart attack.

Trent pounded me on the back. "Take it easy, Chipmunk. Can you breathe?"

I nodded and started my story, but all that came out was a series of tortured wheezes.

"Do you need to go to the hospital?" asked Cal.

I shook my head, gulped back as much air as I could, and rasped, *"Steve Stapleton is too old for the Slapshot League!"*

I could tell I had blown everybody away. The silence was pure shock.

Finally, Trent spoke up. "Coach Wong has been with the Oilers since before we were born. He'd never cheat like that."

"Maybe Coach Wong doesn't know," I panted.

"That's impossible," scoffed Jared.

"Steve's a replacement player," I argued. "When Kenny Gardner got injured, the league probably just called up the first kid on the waiting list. What if they never checked his age?"

Josh raised an eyebrow. "Nobody really knows Steve Stapleton because he goes to County Junior High. Maybe he's in grade eight."

"They go up to grade nine at County," I put in. "They've got kids who are fifteen, even sixteen years old."

"Aren't we forgetting something?" came the quiet voice of the Stars' captain. She turned to face me. "Chipmunk, how do you know Steve's too old?"

"Reporters have ways of finding stuff out," I said

mysteriously. They were unimpressed, so I came clean. "I searched his duffel bag. You know what he had in there? A can of shaving cream."

"Aw, Chipmunk!" groaned Trent. "That doesn't prove anything!"

"Of course it does!" I cried. "How many of you guys shave?"

"None of us," admitted Josh. "But some of the grade sevens do."

"Mike shaves once a week," confirmed Jared. "And Willis Gerard of the Bruins has to almost every day. What about the Leaf's goalie? He's the hairiest kid I've ever seen!"

"Maybe Steve wasn't even using the shaving cream for shaving," suggested Cal. "What if he was going to play a joke on somebody — you know, cream up his locker — or his sneakers — or his *gym shorts*? Yeah, that's funny!"

Cal's got to be the only guy alive who can crack himself up over something that didn't even happen.

I was disgusted. "You guys know nothing about the media. This is big news! The best player in the league is ineligible."

"*If* it's true," put in Josh.

"It's true! It has to be! How come he's so much better than everybody else?"

"Talent?" suggested Trent.

"Wayne Gretzky wasn't this good at our age," I insisted. "Trust me. It's a scoop."

"It's only a scoop when you have proof," Alexia reminded me. "You have a can of shaving cream. You didn't even see a razor, did you?"

"That doesn't mean it wasn't there," I pointed out. "I only got into Steve's bag for a second."

Trent shook his head. "It's tricky, Chipmunk. A lot of people still think that Mars doesn't belong in the Slapshot League. If we accuse Steve, and we're wrong, they'll call us troublemakers. They might even use it against us to force the Stars out of the league for next year."

"I know what we can do," I decided. "In my next column for the *Gazette*, I'll just kind of *hint* that Steve's too old. Then, when Mr. Feldman reads it, *he* can investigate."

"The *Gazette* only comes out once a month," Alexia reminded me. "The next issue won't be until playoff time, when the regular season is over."

I counted the weeks in my head. She was right. This scoop would get Steve kicked out. But by then he'd already *be* out. Everybody would — except the playoff teams.

I threw back my head and howled my frustration

to the sky. "This *stinks*! If I worked for ESPN, I could just go on TV and scoop the whole world!"

They just laughed at me. I could tell they thought I was imagining it all. What's the only thing worse than a scoop you can't use? When no one even believes you!

Trent put a sympathetic arm around my shoulders. "If you worked for ESPN, we'd be in the NHL — not freezing our butts off at an outdoor rink."

"And our fans would do the wave a lot more," added Jared.

Josh shivered. "It *is* cold out here." He signaled to Boom Boom with his goalie stick. "Coach? Is it okay if I go into the warm-up shack for a while?"

"Good idea," Boom Boom approved. "It'll give you a chance to thaw out for a few thingamabobs."

The warm-up shack was the only indoor thing about the Mars rink. It was just a small hut beside the ice. But it had a potbellied stove that was a lifesaver on cold days like this. Mrs. Bolitsky was in there now, baby-sitting the usual pile of shoe boxes.

I handed Guava to Josh. "Since you're going to the day-care center, could you drop mine off?"

"Sure, Chipmunk." He stared at Guava's home, which was built out of plywood. "What's this, a birdhouse?"

"It's an egg-baby protector," I explained proudly.

"I made it in woodshop today. Shoe boxes are kind of flimsy. It's too easy to crush them with your foot or a bus or something."

He headed into the shack, and I turned my attention back to the practice. I recorded a few notes on the different drills, but my mind kept wandering to this Steve business. What a drag! Some reporters spend their whole lives waiting for a scoop like this. To waste it would be a crime against journalism.

I shivered. It didn't help that it was so cold out. Players keep warm by skating and checking and hustling. Reporters just plain freeze. So when Josh came out of the warm-up shack, I took his place with the coach's wife.

It was nice and toasty in there. I felt myself starting to sweat, and it didn't even have anything to do with Mrs. B. To be honest, she wasn't her spectacular self today. There were dark circles under those amazing eyes. Also, she was wearing a baggy sweatsuit instead of her usual supermodel clothes.

I hoped she was okay. I asked Boom Boom about it yesterday at Mars Health Food. He got this weird smile on his face and whispered in my ear, "She's whatchamacallit." But that could have meant tired, sick, faking, or almost anything else!

"Have a seat, Chipmunk," she invited. "I just threw another log on the fire."

"Great, Mrs. B." I frowned at the stack of shoe boxes by the woodpile. "Where's Guava?" She looked blank so I added, "My egg baby. Josh gave him to you."

"No, he didn't," she replied. "Josh just brought in some firewood. There weren't any more shoe boxes."

"Oh, no," I chuckled. "That was my new egg baby. I keep him in a wooden protector. Where is it?"

Mrs. B. looked stricken. She pointed at the stove. "In there."

"*What?!*"

I nearly burned my hand off yanking open the hot iron door. A horrifying sight met my eyes. My egg-baby protector was in flames.

"Are eggshells by any chance fireproof?" I asked hopefully.

A *pop!* and a wisp of gray smoke provided my answer.

. . . *and I'm sure you'll agree it was totally not my fault that Guava exploded.*

     End Caregiver's Log for Egg Baby #4
(Mrs. Spiro — since the last log only took half a page, do I have to buy a whole new notebook for the new one? My allowance was suspended for losing too many egg babies.)

Caregiver's Log for Egg Baby #5
Born: During detention re: Egg Baby #4 (see above)
Name: Van (after Vanilla Swirly-Balls)

"Clarence!" called my mother from the kitchen. "Have you seen the small saucepan?"

Uh-oh. At that moment, the pot she was looking for was sitting on my desk. It was my new and improved egg-baby protector. I called it the "armored shield." Stainless steel is even stronger than wood, and fireproof too. Van was in there, wrapped up in a hand towel that Mom hadn't noticed was missing yet. I had the lid held on with a rubber band.

I stalled. "Can't hear you, Mom!"

I stuck the pot in my backpack and scooted downstairs. "Sorry. Gotta go." And I breezed right past her and out the door.

At Mars Health Food, I piled into the back of the delivery truck with the Stars. A ride in the team "bus" was always an adventure. Did I say ride? It's really more of a bounce. Since I was the only one not wearing hockey pads, I always got banged up the most.

"Wait a minute," I said, looking around. "Where are the egg babies?"

"My dad's baby-sitting," Brian replied.

"So is our mom," put in Josh.

"My grandparents," Cal supplied.

"My sister."

"My aunt."

One by one, the Stars named their caregivers.

"You guys are so lucky," I said sulkily. "My mom thinks Mrs. Spiro is a genius of education. She won't baby-sit because then I'd be shirking my responsibility."

"I agree," Jared told me. "I refuse to trust Wendell to any baby-sitter."

"You mean you just left him at home?" asked Josh. "What are you going to put in your caregiver's log?"

"I didn't *leave* him anywhere," Jared retorted. "Wendell's staying right here with me." He patted his chest. "Tied up nice and safe in the laces of my shoulder pads."

"You mean you're going to *play* with him?" I asked in disbelief. "On the *ice*?"

"He'll never leave my side," Jared said smugly.

"Jared, it's hockey, not Scrabble," Alexia informed her line mate. "One good hit and your egg baby is going to get pulverized."

"That's where you're wrong," Jared chortled triumphantly. "I've got him wrapped in toilet paper. Two-ply."

Well, Cal — he thought that was hilarious. He

started rolling around the truck, flailing his arms and legs while he laughed his head off. I had to duck behind a sack of wheat germ to avoid getting clobbered.

Jared was insulted. "Hey, man, I'm the only one here who's never lost an egg baby! I'm not taking any chances with my perfect record."

Trent was usually waiting for us outside the community center, but today he was at rinkside. It seemed like the whole world was. Midweek night games weren't normally as crowded as the weekend matchups, but today the place was packed. It was Oilers versus Penguins, tied 5–5, in sudden-death overtime.

"Overtime?" I cried, fumbling for my tape recorder. "No way!"

Trent nodded. "Steve Stapleton has all the Oiler goals!"

This story was *huge*! I mean, I knew Steve was awesome. But I didn't think he was so good he could make the lowly Oilers a match for the defending champions. The Penguins had Happer and Oliver — the second- and third-leading scorers in the league. They had the top coach, a tough goalie, and great skaters at every position. They'd only lost one game all year!

Steve was poetry in motion. He cruised down the ice with the grace of a gazelle, but he was also strong enough to send checkers flying. He deked Happer out of his jockstrap and bulled right over Oliver. The arena went as quiet as a library as Steve pulled back his stick for a slapshot.

||||| _Chapter 9_

Pow!

The blistering drive was so hard that you could barely see it. And then the puck hit the mesh of the net behind the Penguins' goalie.

Final score: 6–5, Oilers. It was a major shocker.

The Oilers fans went crazy. Beating the mighty Penguins was almost unthinkable! Not only that, but Steve had just broken the record for most goals in a game. It used to be five, held by — held by —

Uh-oh.

I didn't want to upset Trent, but a reporter can't ignore a big story. "That was six goals, you know," I said softly. "Your record was five."

Our assistant captain shrugged resignedly. "That guy's a lot better than me, Chipmunk. He _deserves_ the record." But he didn't look too happy.

Alexia made a point of being near the gate when Happer and Oliver stomped off the ice.

She flashed them her sweetest smile. "Gee, tough luck, you guys!"

The look she got back from Oliver was pure toxic-waste dump. "It isn't fair! The Oilers were the stinkiest of the stink until they got" — he spat the word — "*him*!"

Trent snickered. There were still a lot of hard feelings between Trent and the Penguins. For him, watching them lose was almost worth having his five-goal mark erased.

"Wipe that grin off your face, Ruben!" Happer snarled at him. "You're the one who's getting bumped from all the record books!"

Trent raised an eyebrow. "Since when do you care about my records?"

"At least you didn't show up out of nowhere," sulked Oliver. "You may not be a Penguin anymore, but you're one of us. We've been in this league together for three years! Did you know this was our hundredth game?"

"No kidding," Trent admitted. "I never counted."

"My uncle keeps all the old schedules," Happer told us. "A hundred games! And Steve Stapleton plays for three lousy weeks, and we have to make him king? Phooey!"

They clattered away.

"All right, you whosises!" called Boom Boom. "Team thingamajig!"

My reporter's sense was tingling as we headed down the corridor. I sensed a whole new plotline taking shape in the story of the Stars from Mars. "Hey, Trent," I asked, "haven't you scored at least one goal in every game you played?"

"Sure, why?"

"Don't you see?" I cried. "You're working on a ninety-nine game scoring streak!"

"So?"

"So if you get a goal today, that'll make a hundred!"

"Hang on, Chipmunk," Trent told me. "Let's not make a big deal out of nothing."

"It isn't nothing," I persisted. "Pretty soon, Steve Stapleton is going to break every record you hold. But a hundred-game scoring streak — that mark would be like the pyramids! No one could ever touch it! Not Steve! Not anybody!"

"If we lose today, we blow our chance to be in the playoffs," Trent said sternly. "We can't get distracted by anything else!"

I kept my mouth shut. But as soon as we got to the locker room, I announced, "Hey, everybody! Trent's on the verge of a hundred-game scoring streak!"

The team was blown away.

"Is that even *possible*?" asked Brian.

We did the math. Thirty games per season, plus playoffs and All-Star tournaments — it added up.

"They ought to give a trophy for that!" breathed Kyle.

"A medal!" added Mike.

"I'll bet our fans will do the wave when they hear about *this*!" added Jared.

"Hey! Hey! *Hey!*" Trent called for quiet. "It's no huge thing!"

"Oh, sure," Alexia said sarcastically. "That's why you got the bigmouth to blab it out to everybody."

Trent shot me a furious look. "I *asked* him to be low-key."

"I *was* low-key," I defended myself, "compared to the article I'm planning to write. How's this for a headline: *Ruben Scores 100 Straight*. Or maybe *The Unbreakable Record*. Or how about *Steve Stapleton, Eat Your Heart Out*?"

"One hundred straight doojigs with a heejazz!" exclaimed Coach Bolitsky. He awarded Trent a pat on the shoulder pads. "That brings back memories! I had a thingamabob like that in my own career."

"Really, Coach?" asked Josh. "You had a scoring streak?"

"Of course not." Boom Boom shook his head. "But

in 1971, I got hit in the face with the puck forty-seven games in a row." He smiled, revealing his three missing teeth. "That's how I lost these dinguses."

Okay, nobody ever said our Boom Boom was a superstar. But I'd like to see Wayne Gretzky absorb a pounding like that and still come up smiling.

It took Trent to bring us back on topic. "We can't let this change our game plan," he insisted. "We have to win today to keep our playoff chances alive. That's the only important thing."

The buzzer sounded to call the teams out onto the ice.

Before I took my seat, I paid a visit to the scorer's table at the penalty box. What luck! Today's arena announcer was Dave — a really good guy who was always nice to the Stars. I filled him in about Trent's scoring streak.

"So when Trent gets his first goal," I finished, handing him a piece of paper, "you'll read this out. Okay?"

"Sure thing, Chipmunk," Dave promised. He took my scribbled speech and placed it under his microphone so it wouldn't blow away.

We were playing the Hot-Dog Heaven Lightning, a team that had no chance of making the playoffs. This wasn't because they stank. It was because their captain got the flu in November and gave it to half the team — who went on to infect the other half. They had to forfeit a lot of games.

They were a tough team, but slow. I could tell that the Stars would be able to skate rings around these guys — especially our speedsters, Brian, Kyle, and Trent. The scoring streak was practically in the bag!

Sure enough, Trent broke free early. He turned on the jets, leaving the Lightning forwards in his dust. He streaked across the blue line before the slower defensemen could scramble into position. Drawing his stick back for a slapshot, he spied Jared hustling down the left wing.

The slapshot never came. Instead, Trent feathered a perfect pass, which Jared tipped into the open corner of the net. 1–0, Stars.

At the scorer's table, Dave whipped out my paper and clicked on his microphone. "Ladies and gentlemen, you have just witnessed hockey history —"

"Not yet, Dave!" I called. "Trent didn't score! That was Jared!"

The microphone clicked off.

The Stars were celebrating, but Jared had his head shoved inside the neck of his jersey, checking on his egg baby. He gave us the thumbs-up signal. Wendell was okay.

The Lightning struck back, evening the game at 1–1.

Then, just before the end of the period, Mike fed the puck to Cal in the slot. The big winger muscled free of a defenseman and golfed a shot between the goalie's legs. 2–1, Stars.

"Ladies and gentlemen," Dave announced, "you have just witnessed hockey history —"

"That was *Cal*!" I shouted at him. "Trent wasn't even on the ice!"

Click.

Titters of laughter buzzed through the crowd.

The locker room was a confident place at intermission. Even though the lead was only one goal, the Stars had turned in a solid all-around performance.

Cal was convinced the team was getting a little extra help today.

"You know," he said slowly, "I'm starting to think that the penny that got frozen into the rink really might be the lucky one."

Alexia groaned and bopped herself on the helmet. "The refs cleaned up two thousand pennies and they missed one. That's all this is."

Cal looked dubious. "I know it sounds crazy, but when I scored that goal, the puck was exactly on top of the penny. If that's not lucky, what is?"

"It's lucky, it's lucky," Boom Boom said quickly. "Now listen up. Here are our second-period thingamabobs."

"Adjustments," I whispered into my tape recorder.

He had some suggestions, but the main game plan didn't change. "We've got these whosises beat," finished the coach. "So get out there and whatchamacallit."

This was one of those times when we really missed Mrs. Bolitsky. She could always translate even her husband's weirdest instructions. I hoped she'd be back soon.

But whatchamacallit — whatever it meant — must have been exactly what the Stars were doing in the second period. It was the same solid play, but at an even higher level of intensity. When the Lightning tried to use their size advantage to slow the game down, the Stars stood right up to them. Alexia and Cal dished out some body checks of their own, and Kyle began his reverse rushes to keep the opposition off balance. When the Lightning did manage to create a scoring chance, Josh was right there to make the save.

I dictated a new headline idea into my tape recorder: *The Slump Is Ancient History.* This was the Stars' best game ever!

There was just one problem. Brian scored on a setup from Jared. Cal notched his second goal of the game on a power play. Alexia stretched the lead to

5–1 with an unassisted masterpiece where she out-muscled a triple team of junior high guys. Get the picture? Everyone was scoring — except Trent! And every single time, Dave the announcer clicked on his microphone and began my prepared speech:

"Ladies and gentlemen, you have just witnessed hockey history —"

And I had to get up and holler, "Not yet, Dave!" What was wrong with the guy? The Stars all had their names on the back of their jerseys, for Pete's sake! What kind of an official scorer doesn't know who scored?

Boom Boom looked at me in perplexity. "What's this thingamajig with you and Dave? Why does he keep babbling about hockey history?"

"I wrote a little speech for when Trent sets the record," I explained. "But Dave keeps messing it up."

Trent glared at me. "Chipmunk, I told you I don't want to make a big fuss about that. Now if I don't score, I'll look like a complete jerk."

"But you *will* score!" I reasoned. "You *always* score!"

Trent shrugged. "We're winning; we're having a great game; who cares who gets the goals?"

"A reporter cares, that's who!" I shot right back. "A good story is everything! Would anybody give a hoot about an explorer if he only sailed six of the seven seas? Or charted three of the four corners of the earth? Well, no one wants to read about a guy who got ninety-nine games into a hundred-game scoring streak! If you're going to make it to the cover of *Sports Illustrated*, you've got to hit the right numbers!"

Before Trent could reply, Mike, our slowest player, scored on a breakaway! A *breakaway*! I mean, the defense could go out for a milk shake and still have plenty of time to come back and stop Mike! He was a human snail!

"Come on!" I hissed at the back of Trent's head. "If Mike can do it, you can too!"

"Ladies and gentlemen," announced Dave. "You have just witnessed —"

"*Shut up!*" It was a chorus from Trent, Boom Boom, and me.

Screams of laughter rang out in the arena.

I held my head. All I wanted was a nice little goal followed by a nice little announcement. Was that asking too much?

║║║║ _Chapter 10_

In the third period, I actually gave up my team reporter's seat behind the bench to go sit with Dave at the scorer's table. I had to keep him quiet until the right moment. By this time, everything he announced was getting belly laughs — even the real stuff. When he reported a goaltending switch for the Lightning, the roar of merriment was so loud that the backup goalie refused to come out of the locker room.

Believe me, my new location wasn't very comfortable in more ways than one. First, Dave was in a lousy mood because he was being laughed out of the arena. Second, there were no extra chairs, so I had to sort of squat on my backpack. I couldn't even put all my weight on it, because Van was in there, protected by my mother's pot. So I perched, sitting, but not really sitting. I thought my legs would break off at the knees. It was agony.

Last but not least, I was getting really nervous. With a big five-goal lead, the Stars went into a defensive shell, and the scoring stopped. How was Trent supposed to get his goal if there wasn't any offense?

I was so frustrated. We were standing on the doorstep of a front-page story, and I was the only one who seemed to care! Sometimes, I think sports would be better off if they kicked out all the athletes and left everything up to the reporters. There'd be a lot more drama. And no one would ever stop a scoring streak at ninety-nine games. That's for sure.

I almost yelled my lungs out. "Come on, Trent! . . . You can do it, Trent! . . . I'm right behind you, Trent! . . . *Darn you, Trent, you're ruining everything!*"

As the minutes ticked down, I squatted there, wallowing in misery and leg cramps. Oh, sure, I knew that the Stars were winning an important game. I knew they were keeping their playoff hopes alive. But I couldn't even bring myself to report on that. It took three years to get to ninety-nine games! If Trent didn't score today, he'd have to start all the way back at zero! What a waste!

"Last minute of play in the game," announced Dave.

Even now, a whole period after anybody scored, he still got a pretty big laugh.

I admit it. I gave up. I just sat there with the handle of my mother's pot digging into my behind, while the greatest story of my reporter's career ticked away.

"He's not going to score," I said out loud. I wasn't talking to anybody. I just needed to hear it myself.

With thirty seconds to play, the Stars were just gliding around, killing time. Suddenly, the Lightning captain stole the puck from Jared and took a wrist shot. Maybe it was because we had a five-goal lead, but Josh was feeling extra confident at that moment. Instead of blocking it with his body, he took a baseball swing at it with his stick.

Thwack!

The puck sailed over everybody's head and plunked down in the neutral zone behind the Lightning defensemen. It bounced once and rolled right up to Alexia and Trent, who had just stepped onto the ice on a line change.

I felt my eyes bulge. It was one of the rarest things in hockey — a double breakaway, two against the goalie!

Alexia snared the puck and sailed down the right wing, flying.

"No-o!" I wailed. "Give it to Trent! *Give it to Trent!*"

And she did. Just inside the blue line, she slipped him a perfect drop pass and veered left to get out of the way of his shot.

Trent must have decided that she had the better angle, because he fed the puck right back to her.

She sent it to him again. "Shoot, hotshot!"

But by this time, Alexia was right at the corner of the net. No hockey player would try to score himself when a teammate was so well-positioned for a tip-in.

So back went the puck from Trent to Alexia.

By this time, the poor goalie was almost crazy from watching them play hot potato.

Ten seconds . . . nine . . . eight . . .

"*Somebody* shoot!" bellowed Boom Boom.

I could read Alexia's face straight through her visor. She'd done everything to set up a goal for Trent Ruben. Enough was enough. Now he was going to get one whether he wanted it or not.

She swooped behind the net and took careful aim — at *Trent*!

Pow!

The puck struck Trent's stick and caromed between the goalie's legs. 7–1, Stars.

I went crazy. This was her play, but it had gone in off Trent's stick. The goal was his. Trent Ruben had a hundred-game scoring streak.

I pounded Dave on the back. "What are you waiting for? This is it! Read the speech!"

"Right!" Dave flipped over a paper and clicked on his microphone. "Would the owner of a blue Volvo please come to the parking lot. Your lights are on."

"No!" I shrieked. "Wrong paper!"

Frantically, Dave grabbed another sheet. He read: "The snack bar will be closing in five minutes —"

"Aw, come on!" I snatched the microphone out of his hand and made the announcement myself:

"Ladies and gentlemen, you have just witnessed hockey history. With that brilliant goal, Trent Ruben has now scored in one hundred straight games. This record will last forever. And you were here to see it."

I paused to give the audience a chance to cheer. Instead, they got up and started for the exits.

"What's the matter with these people?" I demanded.

Dave held up the microphone cable. The plug dangled at the end of it. "You yanked out the wire."

I was horrified. "You mean —?"

"Nobody heard you."

"Quick!" I begged. "Plug it back in! This is important!"

But by that time, the last few seconds of the game had ticked away, and the arena was almost empty.

"Come back!" I pleaded over the P.A. system. "You're missing hockey history! *Awwwwww!*"

In the locker room, a sheepish Trent was accepting congratulations from his coach and teammates.

As the team reporter, I deserved the first interview, especially since this whole record business was my idea.

"How does it feel to be the first player in history with a hundred-game scoring streak?" I asked, sticking my tape recorder in his face.

He looked disgusted. "It feels like a pain in the butt, Chipmunk. And *you're* a pain in the butt for making such a big deal out of it."

It sure is nice to be appreciated.

Alexia strolled over. "Congratulations, hotshot. You never could have done it without me."

Trent had to laugh. "All right, I admit it. I'm happy about the record. But mostly I'm happy that we won and we're only a game away from the playoffs."

Josh stacked his blocker and catching glove on top of his goalie pads. "I'm confused," he said with a frown. "The Panthers lost again today, so they're out of the picture. And the Kings are too far back to make it. So who else has a chance at that number eight playoff spot?"

"Do you think we could have clinched it already?" Cal wondered.

"No," said Trent. "We definitely need one more win."

"Or those other whosises have to lose," put in Coach Bolitsky. He looked around. "Is everybody ready to go? Where's Jared?"

We finally found him at center ice, sitting on the face-off dot, surrounded by his clothes and equipment. He was bent like a pretzel, digging into one shoulder pad.

Boom Boom was shocked. "Jared! What are you doing? Put your whatchamacallits back on!"

"I can't find Wendell!" Jared called anxiously.

"Who's Wendell?" asked the coach.

All at once, Jared's worried face was wreathed in smiles. "Here he is!" From his elbow pad, he produced his egg baby in its cocoon of toilet paper. "Hey, little guy. I was worried about you!"

I'm sure that would satisfy even Mrs. Spiro. Here was a normal kid, sitting half-naked in a hockey arena, burping an empty eggshell.

That's when it dawned on me that I'd better check on Van. Right there at rinkside, I opened up my backpack, undid the elastic, and looked into Mom's favorite saucepan.

"Hooray!"

Van wasn't even chipped. Maybe I was starting to get the hang of this business of being a father.

As I was zipping the backpack shut, my eyes fell on the tote board with the updated league standings.

My breath caught in my throat. All at once, I could see which team had a chance to knock the Stars from Mars out of the playoffs. The Oilers had done so well lately that they were suddenly only half a game behind the Stars. And what team were we playing Saturday to end the season?

Those very same Oilers. It was going to be them or us.

I went over it again and again in my mind. But each time it came out the same way: The road to the playoffs went straight through the great Steve Stapleton.

||||| _Chapter 11_

On Thursday, Waterloo Elementary School was shut down for a teacher conference day. So the league had scheduled a lot of practices at the community center.

As usual, Mr. Feldman gave the Stars the worst time slot — six A.M. He never missed a chance to stick it to us Marsers.

After practice, we all went back to Mars Health Food for breakfast. The meal was gross, of course — bean-curd pancakes with unflavored yogurt instead of syrup. But by this time we were all experts at bypassing our taste buds and wolfing it straight down.

The only problem was Mrs. Bolitsky. She was definitely not feeling well again. I mean, she was there to say hi, and to give us back our egg babies — she was the caregiver *du jour*. But then she had to go take a nap.

You could tell Boom Boom was worried about her. He opened doors for her, pulled out her chair, and wouldn't let her do any of the cooking or cleaning up.

Josh commented on it when the team was alone in the restaurant. "Gee, I hope Mrs. B. is okay."

"Yeah," agreed Kyle. "I never thought I'd say this, but she looks almost kind of — you know — bad."

Alexia snorted in disgust. "You guys are such pigs! She's a little bit under the weather, so she looks like a normal person instead of a magazine cover. That's all you care about — that the scenery's not so pretty! Give her a break. I'm sure she'll be gorgeous again in time for the playoffs."

"The playoffs!" groaned Mike. "We can forget about the playoffs. Steve Stapleton is going to kill us on Saturday!"

"It's not over yet," said Trent. But he didn't look convinced.

I leaped to my feet. "Why doesn't anybody listen to me? That guy is too *old* for the Slapshot League!"

"Chipmunk, we've been over this before," Alexia said in reverse volume control. "There's nothing we can do without proof."

"We can phone Mr. Feldman," I suggested.

"And tell him what?" asked the captain of the Stars. "That you *thought* you saw *shaving cream*?"

"I definitely saw it," I amended.

"It's not enough," said Trent. "We'll just have to do our best against the Oilers."

Did you catch that? "Do our best!" What kind of a bad attitude is that?

But I wasn't through yet. After breakfast, I went straight to the bus stop and headed back into Waterloo. Maybe the Stars were ready to lose their playoff chance, but not the team reporter. The whole Cinderella story was at stake here! Cinderella goes to the ball; she doesn't get cheated out of her ticket by Steve Stapleton!

My plan was simple. Maybe the Stars couldn't approach Mr. Feldman without proof. But his own nephew could. I was sure Happer would jump at the chance to get rid of Steve. The Oilers were the only team that could come between the Penguins and another championship. And without Steve, the Oilers were nothing.

I arrived at the community center just before eleven. Didn't it figure? The beloved Penguins ended up with the perfect practice time. They got to sleep in on teacher conference day, while the Marsers had to crawl out of bed before the roosters.

Coach Monahan really worked the Penguins hard

at practice. And I have to admit they were beautiful to watch, with their precision passes and their power skating. They didn't have anyone as good as Steve, of course. But they had a scoring threat at every position except goalie. More than half of them made the All-Star team year after year.

They greeted me pretty much the way I expected.

"Hey, look, it's the Martian reporter!" Oliver tried to bounce a little flip shot off my nose. Instinctively, I blocked it with Mom's saucepan.

Clang!

Happer charged toward me at top speed. At the last second, he dug in his skates and stopped dead. A shower of snow wafted over the boards and frosted me and my egg-baby armored shield. "Hey, space hick! What brings you to Earth?"

I hesitated. The Stars — my best friends — didn't really believe me about Steve Stapleton. Happer wouldn't either. But maybe there was a way to sort of plant the idea in his head.

"So," I began casually, "what do you think of Steve Stapleton?"

His brow darkened. "That was a fluke last weekend!" he snapped at me. "We can beat the Oilers any day!"

"Isn't it weird how *strong* he is?" I persisted. "I mean, plenty of guys are as big as him, but nobody's half that strong. And his hockey style — I guess you'd have to call it *mature* —"

He was impatient. "What are you getting at, Chipmunk?"

How many hints did I have to drop? Sheesh! Talk about thick as a brick! "— and isn't it funny that nobody knows him?" I went on. "Sure, he goes to County Junior High, but those guys join clubs, and do stuff in town — you know, *with kids their own age* —"

"Hold it!" Finally, there was a glimmer of understanding in Happer's snake eyes. "You think he's too old, right? And you want me to tell my uncle." The eyes narrowed. "Why can't you tell him yourself?"

"Well, I — uh —"

"You don't know for sure!" he reasoned. "You're just guessing! Maybe you're just *hoping*!"

I was babbling by this time. "I — I — I just thought you'd want to ask your uncle to — uh — look into —"

Happer fixed me with a sneer that was like being slapped with a wet fish. "Why should I do that? We're done playing the Oilers. Now it's your turn." He gave a dirty laugh. "Lots of luck."

"You'll have to play them again soon enough," I argued. "They beat you before; they could do it again. And in the playoffs, that means elimination."

He shrugged. "So that's when I'll get my uncle to look into it. But in the meantime, I'll have the pleasure of watching you nebula nerds get booted out of the post-season on Saturday."

And he skated away. "Thanks for the tip, sucker."

I was so mad. Talk about a plan backfiring! Not only was I no closer to getting rid of Steve, but I'd just helped the Stars' worst enemy.

But I wasn't dead yet. What was keeping the Stars from taking action? "You have no proof." Alexia kept saying it over and over. If I could get evidence that Steve was overage, the league would have to declare him ineligible.

I felt a surge of excitement. This was real reporting. How could you prove how old someone is? The town hall kept birth records. But what if he was born someplace else? His doctor would have a file on him, but I didn't have time to phone every doctor in Waterloo. I needed to expose this cheater by Saturday.

And suddenly it came to me: his school. Their file would have everything.

I hauled my pot back to the bus stop. This was the only chance I had to visit County Junior High. Tomorrow I'd be in my own school.

It took three different buses to get there. Once, I forgot Van on the Waterloo Transit and had to run screaming down the road for half a mile before I caught the driver's attention. By the time I got back, I'd missed the regional bus. That meant a forty-minute wait. It was murder!

County Junior High was a giant square building right in the middle of a field. The parking lot was jammed with cars and school buses. But apart from that, there wasn't another sign of human life as far as the eye could see in all directions. I know Mars isn't exactly Times Square, but this place was at the corner of Nowhere Street and Nothing Avenue.

I got a little scared as I went in the front door, holding Van in front of me like I was on my way to a potluck supper. It was a big change from Waterloo Elementary School. I'm kind of small for grade six, and this place was swarming with seventh-, eighth-, and ninth-graders. Some of the grade nines were bigger than my dad.

Luckily, no one looked at me. I almost got stomped on a couple of times, but at least nobody threw me out of the building.

A bell rang. In about two seconds, the halls went from packed to almost deserted. I found the main office and slipped inside.

A secretary fixed me with a suspicious look. "Shouldn't you be in class?" She eyed my pot. "What are you lugging that around for?"

I went blank. "I — I — I —"

Chapter 12 ⎰⎰⎰⎰⎰

My panic was interrupted by a commotion out in the hall. A couple of students started a shoving match at their lockers.

Pretty soon, a chant went up: "Fight! Fight! Fight!"

The secretary rushed out from behind the counter.

"Break it up, you two —"

And there I was, all alone, facing a cabinet that said STUDENT RECORDS. All I had to do was open to the S's. This was easy. If I ever get bored at *Sports Illustrated*, I can always take a side job working for *60 Minutes*.

Simpkins . . . Stanton . . . Stapleton. Jackpot!

The first page confirmed all my suspicions: *Stapleton, Steven. Grade level: 9.*

I knew it! That sneak! That cheat! It takes a special kind of stinker to go up against younger kids just to be a big star! Well, not anymore! Steve Stapleton had played his last game in the Waterloo Slapshot League!

I ripped the paper out of the file and fed it into the copy machine. I was thrilled. I hadn't been in here two minutes and my mission was totally accomplished.

And then a voice called out, "Hey, you! What do you think you're doing?"

A tall man in a dark suit was glaring at me from the doorway of the office marked PRINCIPAL.

Frantically, I ripped the lid off my saucepan. The rubber band snapped and went flying. It hit the principal dead center in the forehead.

"Ow!"

I jammed my photocopy into the pot with Van and ran like a scared rabbit. I slipped by the two fighters in the hall, sprinting for the nearest exit.

Oh, no! Locked!

"Come back, you!" The principal's voice rang out behind me.

I picked a corridor and made a break for it, looking furtively over my shoulder.

Suddenly, a pair of hands reached out and snatched the saucepan away. A teacher with an apron was looking disapprovingly down at me.

"Oh, here you are. You're late. The whole class is

waiting, Kevin." She paused. "You *are* Kevin, aren't you?"

And then I saw the principal rounding the corner. Man, was I ever Kevin! I followed her into the room and made sure the door was shut tight. "Kevin — that's me. You can call me Kev for short."

"Go and get yourself a glass of water, Kevin," she said kindly. "You look like you've run a marathon."

I found a sink — this classroom had six of them! — and poured myself a drink. The teacher went on with the lesson. Now, I don't pretend to understand junior high. But why was she talking about split-pea soup?

"Now we bring the broth to a rolling boil," she was lecturing. "Be careful not to lift the lid and lose the cooking pressure. That will throw off your timing —"

There was a knock at the door. I nearly went through the ceiling. I was afraid it might be the principal coming to get me. But it was just another kid — a kid who also happened to be carrying a pot.

"May I help you?" asked the teacher.

"Is this home ec?" he asked. "Mr. Logan sent me here with the ham stock for your pea soup. I'm Kevin."

Every eye in the room turned to me. But I wasn't watching them. My gaze was riveted on my mom's saucepan. It sat right in front of the teacher, atop a blazing gas burner.

The teacher looked bewildered. "But what's in *this* pot?"

"*Va-a-a-an!!*" I was already running to rescue my egg baby. I grabbed the lid. "Yeow!" It was burning hot, and I dropped it with a clatter. Thick black smoke billowed out of the pot. I didn't want to look inside, but I had to.

The heat had exploded Van into a million pieces. The towel was smoldering. And the edge of my photocopy was on fire. I tried to blow it out, but that only fanned the flames.

Sploosh!

Some hero emptied the fire extinguisher into my mother's pot. The whole room filled with smoke. I dove in with both hands to rescue my sheet of evidence, but the soaked paper disintegrated in my hands.

At that moment, the sprinkler system let go. Water poured down from the ceiling. I made my first sensible move all day: In the confusion, I climbed out the open window. If home ec had been on the third floor instead of the first, it wouldn't have changed my decision.

I didn't stop running until I hit the city limits of Waterloo. That's when it dawned on me that I'd left my mother's favorite pot behind. I made an executive decision to leave it be. It was better for Mom to believe that her saucepan had disappeared off the face of the earth than to find out what really happened.

My mind was in such a jumble that I didn't hear the car come up behind me. The blast from the horn almost put me in the ditch.

I stood there in the weeds and watched it pass by. The large green sign on top read: STUDENT DRIVER.

I goggled. The kid behind the wheel did a double take when he saw me. He recognized me, no question about that. And I certainly recognized him.

It was none other than Steve Stapleton.

▌▌▌▌▌ _Chapter 13_

"Well, it's definite!" I told everyone on the school bus the next morning. "Steve Stapleton isn't just too old. He's _way_ too old. He's sixteen!"

"How do you figure that?" asked Brian.

"He's in driver's ed," I replied. "I saw him yesterday when I went over to County Junior High and photocopied his records. He's in grade nine!"

Everyone on the bus burst into applause.

"Way to go, Chipmunk!" cheered Josh. "Sorry we doubted you."

"Playoffs, here we come!" added Cal.

"_Now_ our fans will do the wave!" exclaimed Jared.

"Have you shown the photocopy to Mr. Feldman yet?" asked Brian.

"Not exactly," I admitted.

"Why not?"

I was tight-lipped. "I kind of lost it in the fire."

"Aw, Chipmunk!" moaned Josh, who wasn't looking forward to facing Steve's slapshot. "You had the proof and you *lost* it?"

"It was the home ec teacher," I accused. "She cooked it."

Josh was wide-eyed. "*Cooked* it?"

"She thought it was soup," I explained miserably. "But this guy Kevin had the real soup —"

Did you ever have one of those true stories where, the more you explain it, the more it sounds like a bad lie? When I got to the part about the sprinklers, I thought they'd throw me off the bus!

"So what you're saying," Alexia commented, "is you've got nothing."

"I *saw* the proof!" I whined. "I *had* it! And I can testify about the driver's ed thing!"

"Where?" she asked sarcastically. "The Supreme Court for hockey cheaters?"

"But it's a hundred percent now!" I cried. "The guy is sixteen! There's no way I made a mistake! When we tell Mr. Feldman —"

"Mr. Feldman hates our guts," Brian interrupted me. "He was one of the guys who voted against letting Mars into the league in the first place. No way he'll listen to us without proof."

"But he'll have to listen to Boom Boom," I argued. "He's the coach *and* the sponsor."

"I can hear it now," laughed Alexia. "'That whosis is too whatchamacallit to play in this thingamabob.' That'll get Feldman's attention."

"Mrs. B. speaks English," I pointed out.

Josh shook his head sadly. "It's the last day before the last game of the season. Without proof, Mr. Feldman would have to investigate on his own. I doubt he could do that before next week. Anyway you slice it, we have to face Steve Stapleton tomorrow. Maybe we can beat him."

The cheer was weak and hollow. In my reporter's heart, I knew the Stars' playoff chances were gone.

But the long faces on the bus were a party compared to the welcome I got from Mrs. Spiro. When I told her about Van, she hit the roof.

She treated me like I was a serial killer, not some poor guy who'd accidentally busted a few stupid eggshells.

"In all the years I've been running the egg-baby project, you are the most irresponsible parent I've ever seen! What if Van had been a real child?"

"But he *wasn't!*" I reasoned.

Wrong answer. Man, was she steamed over one lousy egg baby! Oh, all right — five. From her drawer she took out another egg and placed a pin on the desk beside it.

"This is your last chance, Clarence," she said through clenched teeth. "If anything happens to this egg baby, there will be no others. You will receive an F for this project. Furthermore, you will lose the privilege of doing all your writing assignments on the hockey team and be banned from the *Gazette*."

If I didn't drop dead right then, I'm probably going to live forever.

I don't mind being chewed out. And I've spent more time in detention than in regular class. But this was serious. There are only two things that make Chipmunk Adelman the person he is. One is jawbreakers — and that was gone already, thanks to Mom and the dentist. All I had left was my sportswriting. If I lost it, I might as well disappear.

I blew the yolk out of that egg with the care of a diamond cutter. When I was done, I brought it up to Mrs. Spiro's desk. She wouldn't even look at me.

"Do you want me to paint it?" I asked timidly.

No answer.

"Should I give it a name?"

Nothing. She probably didn't expect this egg baby to make it out the door. What would be the point of naming the poor little soul?

"Okay," I said, talking to myself. "I can do all that stuff at home."

I took a shoe box out of the cupboard. But I knew that wouldn't provide a millionth of the protection I needed for *this* egg baby. My whole writing career could depend on how I handled myself from here on in.

As soon as I got home, I started right to work.

Kwik-Dry Miracle Cement, read the label on the tube. *Goes on liquid, dries harder than concrete in less than five minutes.*

Because the pinholes were small, it took over an hour to fill the entire egg. But when I was done, I had an egg baby that was heavier than a baseball. One thing was definite: Nothing was going to crush this guy.

But as I looked at the thing, I started to worry again. Sure, the inside was as solid as granite. But couldn't the shell just crack off and crumble away? With my sportswriting on the line, I couldn't take that chance.

I went out to the garage and started searching the shelves. I had to find something to reinforce the eggshell.

What was this? *Pavement Sealer.* That was the

black stuff we painted the driveway with last summer. Mom said it filled any cracks and made the surface hard. That was exactly what I was looking for. And we had half a can left.

I pried off the lid and dipped my egg baby into the tarry slop. It came out with a thick black layer on it. I set it down on the can lid to dry and went to wash my hands. Perfect! The stuff didn't come off. I mean, not perfect for my hands. But eggwise, it was great. What could be stronger than a driveway? People park cars there!

I dipped it again. While it was drying, I searched the shelves for one more thing — extra insurance. You know, like wearing a belt *and* suspenders to make sure your pants don't fall down.

And suddenly, there it was. Polyurethane — that's the clear plastic coating we used when we redid the floors a couple of months ago. It wasn't as hard as Miracle Cement, of course. But the good thing about this was you could paint on as many coats as you wanted. The more the better. I put six on there before Mom came out to find me for dinner.

"Clarence, what are you doing? What's all over your clothes?"

My clothes are her number-two pet peeve. (Number one is my teeth. What else?) So while my shirt soaked in paint thinner and my pants went through the heavy soil cycle, she lectured me on how much it costs to dress a twelve-year-old "in this day and age." I never knew Mom was so good at math. She even figured in the sales tax.

I fell back on my last resort — the truth.

"If I kill one more egg baby, Mrs. Spiro says I can't be a reporter anymore."

Good old Mom. She took pity on me. "All right, Clarence. Let's have a look at my grandchild."

We went back to the garage where my egg baby was drying on a shelf.

She was shocked. "That's an egg? *That?* It looks like a grenade!" She picked it up gingerly. "Why is it so heavy?"

"I filled the inside with Miracle Cement," I explained. "It dries harder than concrete, you know."

Her lips twitched. "What's this one's name?"

I thought about it. My favorite black jawbreakers are called Licorice Cannonballs. But it was never a good idea to mention the "J" word when Mom was around.

Besides, there was only one possible name for this shiny black mutant Superman.

"Mom, I'd like to introduce you to Eggzilla, Lord of the Egg Babies."

Chapter 14 \\\\\\

The day dawned gloomy and overcast on the morning of the biggest game in the short history of the Stars from Mars.

The whole season had been building up to this. A single playoff spot remained unfilled. After today, one team would be headed for the post-season. The other would be thinking about next year.

I should have been thrilled. Talk about a *Sports Illustrated* moment! Two teams on a collision course in the last game of the season! Do-or-die hockey! It just didn't get any better.

But this matchup had the sour smell of unfairness. Steve Stapleton, that cheater, was two years too old for this league — and four years older than most of the Stars. Even the Penguins hadn't been able to stop him. And really, how could they? They were twelve, thirteen, and fourteen, same as us. A sixteen-year-old was practically an adult. It would be like a kid playing against Eric Lindros or Paul Kariya.

And if I had put that photocopy into my pocket instead of Mom's saucepan, none of this would matter, because the guy would be gone. I couldn't shake the feeling that it was my fault the Stars didn't stand much of a chance today.

But the first order of business was to prepare a new egg-baby protector. Eggzilla had to come to the game with me, and I sure wasn't going to put him in danger. Shoe boxes are too flimsy; wood burns; we all know the risk when you use a pot; and bullet-proof vests don't come in egg-size.

But I had the perfect thing. We owned one of those giant dictionaries — two thousand pages long. It was almost a foot thick and weighed about twenty pounds. With a steak knife, I hollowed out a small compartment in the middle of the dictionary. In it I placed Eggzilla. It was a perfect fit. When the big book was closed, you couldn't tell there was anything in there but words.

I took an old leather belt and fastened it tightly around the dictionary. Now Eggzilla had it all — strength, security, *and* camouflage. This was more than a protector. This was an egg-baby fortress!

It was a little heavy, though. Which is why I was late getting to Mars Health Food.

"Where *were* you, Chipmunk?" demanded Josh. "The game starts in half an hour! Hurry! Hurry! Hurry!"

All the Stars were nervous like that. Kyle was polishing and repolishing his rearview mirror. Jared had his face buried in his jersey and was carrying on a whispered conversation with Wendell. Brian had chewed clear through the chin-strap of his helmet. Mike had the shakes. Even Alexia — who played it cooler than cool — looked pale and grim.

And if the team was wired, Coach Bolitsky was vibrating like a guitar string. He was running back and forth from the store to the truck, his ponytail snapping like a flag in the wind. His eyes bulged even more than usual out of his praying-mantis head, as he barked instructions at the team:

"Don't forget to bring the dinguses! Have you all got your whatsits? The thingamabob! Who's carrying the thingamabob?"

"Calm down, Boom Boom," soothed Mrs. Bolitsky. "Everybody's got everything. Let's go."

Good old Mrs. B.! Even though she was still under the weather, she was coming along to support the team in this huge game. Of course, there was another angle that no good reporter could ignore.

Maybe she was here because she knew we were going to get clobbered, so this would be the last game of the year. But I didn't say anything to the players. They were scared enough.

At the community center, we met up with Trent, and the Stars headed for their locker room.

Boom Boom put a hand on my shoulder. "Chipmunk, this is a big doojig. Why don't you give us a few whatchamacallits alone before the thingeroo starts?"

"Good idea, Coach. Sure thing." It was right for a team to have a little privacy at a moment like this. A reporter had to respect that.

I switched on my tape recorder and started wandering through the crowd, just to capture the flavor of this big event. The bleachers were already packed. I noticed a lot of shoe boxes scattered throughout the Mars fans. The Stars' parents may have been babysitting, but they sure weren't going to pass up this game.

The Oilers had a large turnout too. They'd been drawing pretty good crowds ever since the coming of you-know-who. They were expecting their team to clinch a playoff spot — and they were probably right.

I ran into Ned and some of the other Oilers in the lobby. They weren't even in uniform yet. I guess they figured they didn't have to do much more than show up to win this game.

As usual, Ned was joking around. "Hey, Chipmunk. Nice dictionary. What are you going to do — look up words between face-offs?"

I laughed too. "Remind me to tell you sometime what this really is. You'll never believe it."

All at once, I froze. There, standing directly in front of me, was Steve Stapleton himself. He didn't look any too pleased to see me. He knew I knew.

He said, rapid-fire, "Come on, guys, let's go to the locker room."

The lobby was so crowded that he was stuck there for a minute. That's how I got a good look at the T-shirt he was wearing under his open coat. It said:

County Elementary School
Grade 6 Graduation
June 20, 1997

Below that was reproduced the autograph of every kid in the class. I could see it as clear as day: *Steven Stapleton.*

My heart started pumping double speed. I didn't need my lost evidence that Steve was overage. This boob was stupid enough to bring along his own evidence and wear it right across his chest! If he graduated from grade six three years ago, that put him in grade nine today!

I set out to find Mr. Feldman.

He wasn't in the office, but I caught him heading for the bleachers with a couple of other league officials.

"Mr. Feldman! Mr. Feldman! Come quick!"

The league president's eyes turned in my direction. He frowned. When he looked at me, he didn't see a reporter with a breaking news story. He saw a Martian.

"The game is about to start," he said shortly.

"But this is *about* the game!" I pleaded. "It's not fair! The Oilers —"

"Put it in a letter," he interrupted. "Everything has to be in writing. That's league policy."

And he turned his back on me and continued to his seat.

"Steve Stapleton is *sixteen*!" I bellowed after him.

But my words were lost in the hubbub of the large crowd.

There is no more terrible feeling than not getting justice when you know you're right.

I ran up to the scorer's table. "Dave! Am I glad you're working today! You have to make an announcement for me!"

Dave glared at me. "Beat it, Chipmunk. I'm in enough trouble after last week."

"But it's urgent!" I begged. "Here — give me the microphone! I'll do it myself!"

He was furious. "No way. I'm fired if I let you anywhere near this P.A. system."

"*Awwwwww!*"

Using my dictionary as a blocker, I plowed through the milling hockey fans to the Stars' locker room. Yeah, Coach Bolitsky had asked for privacy. But with the playoffs on the line, there was just too much at stake here.

I burst in the door and blurted, "I've got more proof that Steve's too old!"

Josh leaped to his feet. "Proof? Where?"

"He's wearing it!" I described the T-shirt in detail. "All we have to do is show it to the referee!"

Boom Boom shook his head. "That won't work. The only thingamajig I can challenge an opposing forward on is his heejazz."

"His stick," Trent translated. "That's in the rules. We can't ask the referee to look under his jersey."

I thought hard. "I know. One of you guys will have to pull off his sweater so the ref can see the T-shirt underneath!"

The coach was horrified. "Absolutely not! That would look like whatchamacallit!"

"Like fighting," Trent agreed. "And if you get

called for fighting, you're not only out of the game; you're out of the league. For life!"

Alexia spoke up. "I know you're only trying to help, Chipmunk, but it just isn't going to happen."

Boom Boom ruffled my hair. "Thanks anyway, kid."

I was destroyed! Devastated! This was like admitting there is no such thing as fairness, and that crime always pays in the end.

"*I'll* do it," I said suddenly.

"You?" chorused half the team.

"Why not?" I demanded. "I'll put on the spare uniform, rent skates, borrow equipment, and I'm there."

"But you can barely skate!" protested Cal.

"I'm not going to play the whole game!" I argued. "I'll line up out there, they'll drop the puck, and I'll pull the guy's shirt off! Who cares if they kick me out of the league? I was never in it!"

"That's the problem," put in Josh. "You're not a Star. That makes you just as illegal as Steve Stapleton."

"Not true," said Boom Boom thoughtfully. "When I first filled out the forms to sponsor a thingie, I was afraid the league would say we didn't have enough whosises. So I signed up every boy in Mars who was the right age. See?"

He flipped through his clipboard and pulled out the team's pre-season proposed roster. Our two captains, Alexia and Trent, weren't even on the list yet. But there it was, at the top of the page: *Adelman, Clarence*.

I turned back to Boom Boom. "You've got to let me do this, Coach! It's the only way!"

The praying-mantis eyes whirled as Boom Boom thought it over. Then he said, "Suit up, Chipmunk."

Chapter 15

Scared? I thought I was going to die!

First of all, if I'd wanted to be a hockey player, I never would have become a reporter. And second, Steve Stapleton was four years older than me. When I pulled off his jersey, he was going to pull off my head.

Trent was thinking the same thing. "Don't be a hero, Chipmunk," he advised as we skated our warm up. "Just get the job done and then drop flat on the ice. The rest of us will call the referee."

"Good idea," I agreed. "Hey, listen, Trent. I left Eggzilla under the bench. I should be out of this game in the first few seconds. But just in case it somehow gets back to Mrs. Spiro, you were the baby-sitter, okay?"

He grinned. "Sure thing. After what you're doing

for us, the whole team would be happy to sign for you."

There was a murmur among the Mars fans. I know they were commenting on "Who's the new guy?" All the other Stars had their names on their jerseys. And there I was, number thirteen — nobody.

The referee blew his whistle to call the teams to the circle. This was it!

I lined up at center so I could be the closest to Steve. I almost swallowed my mouth guard as he took the position on the other side of the face-off dot. He wasn't huge, but I'm kind of shrimpy. And *parts* of him seemed larger than life! Both my feet could have fit inside one of his skates! His head was twice the size of mine! A crazy thought occurred to me: I gave up jawbreakers for nothing. Because if this guy knocked my teeth out, what difference would cavities make?

And then the puck was dropped.

I let go of my stick and made a grab for Steve's jersey. It wasn't there. *He* wasn't there. He was already roaring across the blue line.

"Hit him!" bellowed Boom Boom from the bench.

Brian came from one side; Kyle backed in from the other.

Crash!

Steve stopped short and let them bodycheck each other.

Wham!

Alexia got her shoulder into Steve's ribs. He just shook her off and kept skating. Trent tried from the other side and missed.

Steve roared in on Josh and put a wrist shot over his shoulder. 1–0, Oilers.

By the time all the players came back to the face-off circle, I still hadn't succeeded in picking my stick up off the ice. It's almost impossible with those big clunky gloves, you know.

"This may not be as easy as I thought," I whispered to Alexia.

Her reply was so reverse volume control that I didn't catch it.

Face-off!

This time I didn't drop my stick. I just grabbed a fistful of jersey and held on tight. Then I managed to get a good grip with the other hand. I was about to start undressing the guy when I noticed I was speeding up.

I kid you not — he towed me from center ice all the way to Cal's lucky penny, which was the spot where I fell. So I had the best seat in the house — with my nose in the goal crease — to see Steve's second score of the day. It was a beautiful deke, with a little flip that beat Josh on the stick side.

When I got up again, the referee was pointing at me. "Number thirteen, two minutes for holding."

"That wasn't holding!" I complained. "That was hanging on for dear life! If I let go, I would have ended up in the parking lot draped over a lamp-post!"

He tacked on another two minutes for unsportsmanlike conduct. A reporter is supposed to question things; a hockey player had better keep his mouth shut.

Boom Boom came over to the side of the penalty box. "Are you still up for this, Chipmunk?" he asked in concern.

I took a look at that cheater, Steve, accepting the worship of Ned and his teammates. It straightened my backbone. "You bet I am, Coach. I'll get the job done. I promise."

Meanwhile, the Stars had a double penalty to kill. Trent won the face-off and drew the puck back to Brian. Brian passed across to Kyle, who redirected it to Alexia.

All at once, I understood. They were playing keepaway. Coach Bolitsky must have decided that there was no stopping Steve Stapleton, so the only answer was to keep the puck away from him.

Eventually, Steve's line went to the bench, and the Oilers' second unit came on. You could see the difference right away. Without Steve, the Oilers were weak. Trent, Alexia, and Company got a much-needed rest. Our other line hit the ice to kill off what was left of my four minutes.

Steve didn't come back until my penalty was nearly over. Immediately, Boom Boom sent Alexia to check the guy. The puck was in our end, with Alexia and Cal double-teaming Steve in the corner. They were both great diggers, but Steve was so strong that it took Jared's help, and finally Trent's, to golf the puck out of our zone.

The timekeeper tapped me on the shoulder. "Penalty's up."

I stepped out onto the ice — just as the puck came bouncing over the blue line. It landed right on my stick.

Okay, I was only out there to undress Steve Stapleton. But I couldn't pass up a clean breakaway.

I took off at top speed, legs pumping, heart pounding. And I found out that my top speed isn't very top at all. In fact, I was totally exhausted before I made it to the Oilers' blue line. But I kept on going, gasping and stumbling. Somehow, the puck came with me.

I heard Boom Boom's voice: *"Look out!"*

That was when Steve caught up with me from behind. Amazing! The guy had crossed the full length of the ice in the time it took me to go twenty feet.

He poke-checked the puck from me like I wasn't even there. It rolled to the Oilers' goalie, who got ready to clear it.

Suddenly, I realized I was right next to Steve. I turned around and started yanking on his sweater.

The goalie fanned on his clearing pass. Trent blocked it with his body just inside the blue line, and took a booming slapshot.

"Owww!" I cried.

The blistering drive struck me right in the seat of my hockey pants and deflected into the Oilers' net.

IIIII Chapter 16

The Mars fans went crazy, and so did the Stars. They were patting me on the back and congratulating me. That's when it hit me — since the puck had bounced in off *me*, I was the goal scorer!

"Way to go, Chipmunk!" cheered Cal. "That's using your head!"

"I didn't score it with my head," I tried to explain. "It went in off my —"

"We saw," interrupted Boom Boom. "It was your heejazz."

Right. And my heejazz was plenty sore.

Anyway, you're probably expecting to hear that we figured out how to stop Steve Stapleton, and went on to control the game. Well, forget it. Nobody our age stops Steve Stapleton. Not even with a force field from *Star Trek*.

In the first period, the Oilers had twenty shots on net, and eighteen of them were from Steve. Josh was making some pretty impressive saves. But Steve got off one slapshot that was so hard I don't think Josh even saw it. Maybe that was a good thing. If our goalie had tried to block it, the puck might have gone straight through him. The Oilers led 3–1 at intermission.

My job — getting Steve's jersey off and exposing his age to the referee — was a total disaster. Most of the time I felt like I was on a tricycle, trying to catch up with a Corvette.

In the second period, Boom Boom sent me out there for one last chance.

"Sorry, Chipmunk," he told me. "We can't waste the whole whatchamacallit trying to do a thingamabob that just isn't working."

"It's okay, Coach. I understand." And I did. But I felt terrible.

I chased Steve all over the ice before I finally got myself tangled up in his jersey just outside the Oilers' crease.

Alexia broke free of a check and fired a hard wrist shot.

Clang!

"Oof!"

The puck hit the post, ricocheted off my stomach, and rolled between the goalie's legs.

That's how I got my second goal of the game. And a bruise to match the one on my heejazz.

Boom Boom was laughing when I got back to the bench. "I can't take you out! You're our leading scorer!"

"You know how you did that?" asked Cal. "It was my lucky penny. You were standing right over it when you scored."

Trent was excited. "I don't know how it's happening, but we're right in this game. If we can stay with them, maybe we'll catch a break."

Jared jumped right on that. "I know what'll put us over the top!" He leaped up on the bench and faced the crowd. "The wave!" He began demonstrating. "Do the wave!"

He got a lot of curious looks, but no wave.

"We won't need the wave," I assured him, "because I'm going to expose that cheater to the world!"

But my promise was empty. I never got anywhere near Steve Stapleton, and neither did the other Stars. He skated everything but figure eights out there. The only goal he didn't score himself he set up so perfectly that Ned would have had to be asleep to miss it. Before you could blink, it was 5–2.

Then, miracle of miracles, the Stars got a power play. As a penalty killer, Steve had to stay put in the "box" formation. I knew I'd never have a better chance than this. I grabbed two fistfuls of jersey and heaved with all my might. In the struggle, my head ended up inside his sweater.

"What's the *matter* with you, kid? Are you *crazy*?" his voice rumbled under there.

What I couldn't see was Kyle, skating in from the point on a reverse rush.

Crash!

He backed right into us. Steve barely moved, but I dropped out of there like a stone. As I plowed into the ice nose-first, the bottom bar of my face mask struck the edge of the puck. It flipped up like a tiddlywink and sailed end over end past the goalie.

5–3, Oilers.

In the locker room at the second intermission, I turned on Kyle. "Don't you look in that rearview mirror of yours?" I demanded. "I had his sweater almost all the way off when you hit us! You spoiled everything!"

Kyle was mystified. "But you *scored*! You completed a hat trick!"

"We'll get more goals than we know what to do with when that big cheater is gone!" I raged.

I admit it. I was wrapped up in the game. But I

was still enough of a reporter to listen in on Coach Wong of the Oilers as he made his speech at the start of the third period. It was about cooperation and teamwork, and how they were all in this together.

But once the players stepped out on the ice, Ned slapped Steve on the shoulder pad. "The whole team can smell the playoffs! Get out there and win it yourself!"

Steve skated off, grinning.

I won't try to sugarcoat it. He killed us. Picture Steve zooming around the ice with two or even three checkers hanging off him. We weren't strong enough or good enough. And we definitely weren't old enough.

By the time the period was half over, Steve had another pair of goals, which brought the score to 7–3. The last was on the hardest slapshot I've ever seen. Josh actually gloved it, but it still carried his hand backward over the goal line. Steve had already equaled his single game scoring mark. He was on the verge of breaking his own record.

"Do the wave!" Jared howled at the crowd. "Can't you see how much we need the wave?"

I had a new plan. I was never going to get Steve's jersey over his head. Now I was just going to rip it straight off. And since Steve was always in the heart of the play, so was I.

That's probably why Brian's shot from the point glanced off my elbow and went into the net. I got a nasty welt from that one. Or why Cal's botched wraparound deflected in off my knee. Large bump, very painful.

With a minute to play, I was trying to tear a hole in Steve's sweater, when a stinging slapshot went off both my ankles. Now the lead was 7–6, and I was black and blue in stereo.

The fans were going nuts, half cheering, half laughing. I mean, I'd scored six goals, and not one of them had so much as touched my stick! I had the wounds to prove it!

The Oilers called time-out and gathered around their bench for a conference. My reporter's ears eavesdropped.

"It's that little kid, Coach!" Steve complained. "Number thirteen! We've got to find a way to shut him down!"

"Are you kidding?" cried Coach Wong. "He's the worst player I've ever seen! He looks like he can barely stand on his feet!"

"That's all an act!" Steve insisted. "He's a ringer! Nobody could be that bad!"

Alexia overheard too. She grinned at me. "Don't be insulted, Chipmunk," she whispered. "We all know you're that bad."

Boom Boom's praying-mantis eyes were whirling again. But he couldn't think of a single piece of advice for this situation. After all, what can you tell a team with six goals, all of them by mistake?

"Chipmunk," he said finally, "keep doing the same whatsits you've been doing."

"But I haven't been doing any whatsits!" I protested.

The coach seemed happy with that. "Exactly," he approved. And at that moment, the referee called the teams back onto the ice.

"What does he mean?" I asked the other Stars as we lined up for the face-off.

Nobody answered. In fact, the whole arena had gone quiet. Fifty-eight seconds remained on the clock. The Stars trailed by a goal. The playoffs hung in the balance. This was it. Crunch time. Most reporters only wrote about it. But here I was, in the middle of it all.

I'll never forget that feeling!

Chapter 17 \ \ \ \ \ \

Trent was the picture of concentration as he squared off opposite Steve. But the sixteen-year-old's eyes were on me.

"You're good, kid," came the New York City cop voice. "But I'm better."

Trent and Alexia laughed in his face.

He was enraged. "What's so funny?"

"Chipmunk's going to get you!" Alexia taunted.

"You don't have a prayer against Chipmunk!" Trent chimed in.

"Are you crazy?" I hissed at them. "What are you doing?"

"Chipmunk?" Steve repeated. He stared into my face mask. "I know you! You're that reporter kid who's been following me! What do you want from my life?!"

"Well, for starters, you could play against people your own age —" I began angrily.

"Hey! *Hey!*" snapped the ref. "Cut it out, you two!"

I could tell Steve was pretty flustered, because he blew the face-off. Trent's quick stick snatched up the puck. He danced over center and shot it into the Oilers' end. Both teams chased after it. I chased Steve.

"Fifty seconds!" bellowed Boom Boom from the bench.

An Oiler defenseman picked up the puck in the corner, but Alexia leveled him with a shoulder check. She passed to Kyle, who took a blast from the point.

The goalie made a sharp stick save. Brian slashed in and pounced on the rebound for a snap shot.

Another save! A forest of sticks slashed at the bouncing puck.

Why wasn't Steve going for any of these rebounds? Come to think of it, where was he?

I caught a flash of Oiler blue over my shoulder. Steve! *He* was tailing *me*! He thought I was *good*!

"I'm lousy!" I shrieked, wheeling to grab at his jersey. I lost my balance and fell flat on my face. Dazed, I scrambled back up. "See?"

Ned had the puck, but Trent deftly poke-checked it away. He raised his stick to shoot.

The foghorn voice of Boom Boom Bolitsky carried over from our bench. "Shoot the dingus at Chipmunk!"

"What?!"

It wasn't just me. It came from our whole team, and half the Oilers too.

"Shoot it at Chipmunk!" the coach yelled again.

And then Trent Ruben — my teammate, my *friend* — pivoted and launched a booming slapshot right at me.

I ducked.

Clannnnng!

The drive slammed right into my face mask. I'm amazed the vibration didn't shake all my teeth loose. But the puck didn't bounce off. It was wedged between the bars of my cage!

It blotted out the whole game. All at once, I was blind.

"*Get that kid!*" howled Steve.

Man, did he get me. Picture it: Sixteen-year-old Steve Stapleton smashing into just-turned-twelve-and-not-even-a-real-player Chipmunk Adelman. It was the body check to end all body checks.

Wham!!

I felt like I was being struck by an express train. All the little points of pain from my six goals came together in one big hurt. The hit was so hard that my head snapped forward. The collision jarred the puck loose from my face mask. It blooped out over the goalie's outstretched pad, under his glove, and into the net.

"Oof!"

Man, that post was hard. I staggered off right into the arms of Trent.

I was enraged. "You did that on purpose!"

But he was howling with joy. "Way to go, Chipmunk! You tied the game!"

The Mars fans were so loud I thought the roof would come down. Kyle took a backward leap at us, bowling us over. Brian piled on.

The P.A. system sprang to life, and Dave's voice echoed in the arena. "Ladies and gentlemen, you have just witnessed hockey history. Chipmunk Adelman has scored seven goals in one game — and the snack bar will be closing in five minutes."

There was a lot more laughing than cheering, but it felt pretty good anyway. The important thing was our playoff hopes were still alive. The Stars and Oilers were twenty-nine seconds away from overtime!

Coach Bolitsky called me over to the bench and sent Mike out to help kill the remaining time.

Cal, who was fiddling with a ripped suspender, slapped me on the back. "Way to go, Chipmunk!"

"That hurt!" I complained. "I had a puck bounce off there, you know!"

"You had a puck bounce off *everywhere*!" laughed Cal. He frowned. "Coach, how can I fix this suspender?"

But Boom Boom was too engrossed in the game to deal with equipment problems. "We've got the whatsit!" he declared.

His players on and off the ice stared in confusion.

"The momentum?" questioned Trent.

Boom Boom shook his head. "The whatsit! You know — the doojig!"

"The strategy?" asked Alexia.

"The wave?" offered Jared.

I took a stab at it. "The advantage?"

"Yes!" The coach snapped his fingers. "Remember, we're ahead in the standings by half a thingamajig! In overtime, win or tie, we make the playoffs! Those whosises have to beat us!"

We sat up taller on the bench. On the ice, the players' skate blades flashed a little brighter. You could almost smell the hope. Could this be the light at the end of the long dark playoff tunnel?

And then everything fell apart.

Trent lost the face-off; Alexia dropped her stick; Mike's skate came off; and for some crazy reason,

Brian went backward and Kyle went forward and they both went down.

The Stars and their fans watched in agony as Steve roared in on net all alone. Poor Josh was shaking so badly that I could actually hear his goalie stick drumrolling against the ice.

This was it — the end of the greatest Cinderella story I would ever see. I couldn't help it. I shrieked my frustration to the world. "No-o-o-o-o!!"

Just outside the crease, Steve began his deke. And suddenly, his skates slipped right out in front of him. The great Steve Stapleton, the best skater in the league, fell flat on his back. The puck slid harmlessly behind the net.

I thought Boom Boom would go through the roof. "He tripped!"

"He tripped over *nothing*!" I added breathlessly.

Cal dropped the belt he was using to repair his suspender strap. He gawked at where Steve had gone down. "It wasn't nothing!" he said with reverence. "He tripped over — *my lucky penny*!"

Jared climbed back up on the bench. "It's time for the wave! The wave!" As he bent down to demonstrate for the fans, a small green object dropped out of the neck of his jersey and rolled along the bleachers.

Horror widened his eyes. *"Wendell!"* he croaked, throwing up his hands in agitation.

That caught the attention of Mr. Gunhold in the stands. "Hey!" he shouted, pointing at Jared. "I think he wants us to do the wave!"

A few parents got the message. They stood and raised their arms. "Do the wave!"

"No! Don't do the wave!" screamed Jared. "Not *now*! You'll crush Wendell!"

But it was catching on. First the Mars fans, and then the Oilers fans, too, rose in rhythm. Up went their arms, and down again, as the wave circled the arena.

"Stop waving!" begged Jared. "Watch your feet! Awwwww —"

He dove off the bench onto the bleachers. There he began crawling after his lost egg baby, getting kicked and jostled by the spectators as they continued their wave.

"Jared!" barked the coach. "Get back on the thingamabob!"

But there was no time to chase after his wandering winger. Eighteen seconds remained on the clock.

Alexia chased the puck down in the corner. Ned was hot on her heels. She hacked at it with a mighty golf swing, but Ned's stick was in the way. The clearing pass soared high into the arena lights.

There was a stampede for the neutral zone. Ten hockey players skated and fought for position, trying to predict where the flying puck might come down.

And in the middle of everything, I had a sudden devastating vision. The belt that Cal had used to fix his suspenders — *it was the one from Eggzilla's dictionary!*

Chapter 18 \ \ \ \ \ \

My eyes shot to the floor under the bench where I'd left my egg-baby fortress. My heart caught in my throat. There was nothing there.

Then I heard the coach's voice. "What kind of a whosis brings a whatchamacallit to a hockey game?"

I stared in horror. Boom Boom had the dictionary in his hands.

"Coach!" I gasped. "No!"

But I was too late. The big book flopped open and Eggzilla rolled out over the boards.

The coach's eyes widened. "A doohickey?"

"My egg baby!"

At that very moment, Alexia's clearing pass dropped to the ice. And suddenly, *two* round black objects stood out against the white of the neutral zone.

There was a split second of shocked silence. Then — war!

Sticks hacked, skates kicked, shoulders checked. Trent won the fight for one "puck"; Steve had the other. Both players streaked for the opposing nets.

"Don't shoot!" I yowled. "One of you has Eggzilla!"

But I knew they had to. Only three seconds remained in the game.

Like mirror images of each other, Trent and Steve pulled back their sticks.

Pow! *Pow!!*

Trent's slapshot was a low sizzler that beat the goalie between his pads. But Steve's was a missile. It ripped clear through the mesh behind Josh and shattered the glass at rinkside.

Both red lights flashed on. I couldn't believe it! Even *Sports Illustrated* never had a story like this! Two goals at the same instant!

The question was: Which had been scored with the real puck?

It almost tore me in two. Part of me prayed for Trent's goal to be the one that counted. That would mean an 8–7 victory, and a playoff spot. But it would also mean that poor Eggzilla had just blasted through a sheet of three-quarter-inch protective glass. No egg baby — not even Eggzilla — could survive a collision like that.

Both sides were celebrating. But I was already off the bench, hightailing it to the Stars' net.

Josh had his mask flipped up, revealing a bewildered expression. "Chipmunk, what happened?"

"Two pucks!" I yelped. "Well, actually, only one *real* puck —" There was no explaining it.

I skated behind our torn net. The glass panel was gone like it had vanished into thin air.

"That could have been my head!" Josh said feelingly.

I peered over the boards — and goggled. There, in the shadow of the Zamboni, sat a round, black —

My heart soared. "Eggzilla!"

And he was *one hundred percent okay*!

Unbelievable! This egg baby had shattered shatterproof glass! It had put a *dent* in the parked Zamboni! And here it was in one piece.

They weren't kidding when they called that stuff Miracle Cement! This was an A-one bona fide miracle!

"Josh!" I howled. "We won!"

The Stars — the league joke, the team nobody wanted — these Cinderellas from Mars had earned the right to play for the championship against the very best Waterloo had to offer!

The referee reached into the Oilers net and pulled out the real puck. He raised his arm to signal a goal for the Stars.

I started cheering. Let me tell you, I was a banshee, shrieking at the top of my lungs. *"We did it! It was the most amazing, fantastic, unbelievable, stupendous —"*

That's when I noticed we weren't alone behind the Stars' net. Steve Stapleton was watching us.

"Kid," he said to me, "you're not much of a skater; you don't play your position; and you can't shoot at all. But you're always where you have to be to make the big play. You've got the greatest puck sense I've ever seen. I knew what you were going to do, and I still couldn't stop you." He held out his hand.

I shook it. "You're not so bad yourself." Suddenly, I remembered the tradition in Olympic hockey — how two players who respect each other exchange souvenirs after a hard-fought battle. "Hey, I know. Let's switch jerseys." I pulled off my Stars uniform and held it out to him.

"It's a deal!" he exclaimed.

But as soon as he had his sweater over his head, I screamed, "Ref! *Ref!!*" And when the official skated up, I pointed at Steve's T-shirt. "Look at this! If he was in grade six three years ago, that puts him in grade nine today! He's too old to play in this league!"

Steve stared at me. "What are you, nuts? You're in the playoffs! Our season is over! What's the point of getting me kicked out *now*?"

"Exposing the truth," I explained with satisfaction. "There's nothing more important to a reporter."

"Well, son," the ref said to Steve. "Why don't you explain how this T-shirt doesn't mean what I think it means."

Naturally, Steve tried to hem and haw his way out of it. But the ref was no dummy. He called Mr. Feldman onto the ice to make the official ruling. And when the league president asked Steve to come back with his parents and his birth certificate, Steve confessed the whole thing.

"Okay, I was on the Slapshot League waiting list," he admitted, shamefaced. "But it was from two years ago, when I was in seventh grade." He shrugged. "I guess someone forgot to delete my name. So when I got the call to replace some kid who broke his leg, I figured, What the heck? Kind of a goof, you know? But then we started winning, and —" His voice trailed off.

"Who else knew about this?" demanded Mr. Feldman.

"Coach Wong had no idea," Steve said quickly. "I think some of the players might have suspected something. But they never asked, and I never told. Like I said, it was all a joke."

"This 'joke' could get you banned from Waterloo sports for life, young man!" fumed the league president.

The Stars lifted me up on their shoulders for a victory lap around the rink. I got a standing ovation. For sure everybody thought I was being honored for my seven goals. But this wasn't about scoring. It was about justice. Steve Stapleton was going to get what he deserved.

Only a jawbreaker could have made this moment more perfect. The Stars were *in*. Steve was *out*. Nothing was missing. Nothing except —

"Wait a minute," Josh said suddenly. "Where's Jared?"

From my vantage point atop everyone's shoulders, I scanned the community center. I finally spotted our winger in the bleachers among the thinning crowd. He was on his knees, white as a ghost and crying.

I squinted. His cupped hockey gloves cradled a few broken green fragments.

Wendell.

Chapter 19 \\\\\\

The egg-baby project officially ended on Monday morning. Before we left English class, we had to hand in our journals and our egg babies so Mrs. Spiro could grade them.

Jared delivered what was left of Wendell in a Ziploc sandwich baggy. "I'm a terrible parent," he croaked. He was so upset that I was afraid he might start bawling again. "I was only trying to do what was best for Wendell. And look what happened."

Mrs. Spiro put an arm around his shoulders. "There, there, Jared. This is what egg babies are all about — to let you feel the *responsibility* of being a parent. You've done that more than any student in this school. I'm giving you an A-plus for the project!"

Well, what do you know! After three weeks of

treating these eggshells like a life-and-death business, Mrs. Spiro was finally chilling out. Jared walked off with his head held high, and the rest of us zipped through the line.

Except for me.

"Hold it right there, Clarence."

The teacher was looking at Eggzilla like I had just placed a tarantula on her desk.

So I gave her the whole story. You know, the Miracle Cement, the pavement sealer, and the polyurethane. She wanted parent responsibility? I had parent responsibility up the wazoo. When I got through being responsible, Eggzilla was so protected that not even a Steve Stapleton slapshot through shatterproof glass could hurt him.

She was furious. "This goes beyond anything, even for you, Clarence! To take a *baby* and fill it with poisonous chemicals and then seal it up so it can't breathe —"

"But eggshells don't breathe —" I pointed out.

She kept talking right over me. "— to do what you did — why, that's almost — almost —" She fixed me with horrified eyes. "Why, that's almost *criminal*! I'm giving you a D-minus for this project. And you can thank your lucky stars you didn't get an F!"

Isn't that just like a teacher? Talk about missing the point! I took a fragile eggshell and made it *invincible*! And all she cared about was a little poison.

But I didn't mind. After all, a D-minus is a pass. Which meant I could still write for the *Gazette*. It was a good thing too. The Stars from Mars were playoff-bound. And Chipmunk Adelman, reporter, would be with them every step of the way!

The last Stars meeting of the regular season took place in the Enochs' backyard. It wasn't about hockey at all. Jared was burying Wendell. And we were all invited, including the coach and his wife.

"A funeral for an eggshell," commented Alexia as we gathered around the hole in the corner of Mrs. Enoch's vegetable garden. "If this isn't the most idiotic thing I've ever been a part of, it's close."

Trent pointed to the tiny wooden marker that stuck out of a small mound of earth next to the grave. "What's that?"

"Jared's goldfish," Josh whispered. "Wendy."

Since I was standing with the team captains, I decided it was time to bring up the subject that had been bothering me since the Oilers game.

"Listen," I began. "I know I scored all those goals and was the MVP and all that. But I really can't join the Stars full-time. I'm just too busy as the team reporter. Sorry, guys."

Trent, Alexia, and Josh stared at me like I had a cabbage for a head.

"Don't worry about *that*, Chipmunk," Alexia told me. "Nobody wants you on the Stars."

"But —" Honestly, I thought they would at least give me an argument! "But I scored seven goals! I set the record! I made hockey history!"

"This kind of thing happens in sports," chuckled Trent. "It was a fluke, like getting struck by lightning or winning the lottery. You could never do it again in a million years."

"It's great that you feel that way, Chipmunk," added Josh. "We were afraid you might expect to join the team. Nobody wanted to hurt your feelings when we had to say forget it."

Is that ungrateful, or what? I mean, I didn't want to be a player. But they could have begged and groveled a little! Especially after I helped them make the playoffs. "Thanks — I think," I mumbled under my breath.

Jared stood up. "Well, we're all here to say good-bye to Wendell. I know he wasn't a real person. But he was a good egg baby, and I'll miss him." He turned to Boom Boom. "Coach?"

I think Boom Boom was daydreaming, because it took an elbow from Mrs. B. before he said, "Hmmmm?"

"Wouldn't you like to say a few words?" Jared asked expectantly. "You know, on behalf of the team?"

"Oh, sure. Of course." The praying-mantis eyes whirled like pinwheels as he wracked his brain for a fitting comment.

"Wendell was a great doohickey," he began. "His courage and his thingamajigs were an inspiration to us all. A lot of whatsits will go by before we see another doohickey like him."

"Let's have a moment of silence to think about that," suggested Jared.

Personally, I didn't think a *year* of silence would be enough time to figure out what the coach had just said.

I heard a couple of snickers during the tribute, but nobody totally cracked up. Not even when Alexia whispered, "May he rest in pieces." Cal had to bite his tongue after that one, though.

Jared placed Wendell's Ziploc baggy into the hole, and we all took turns dropping handfuls of dirt on top.

Mrs. Bolitsky was last. Suddenly, all the color drained from her face, and she gave a little gasp. She didn't exactly fall, but she sat herself down on the grass beside the vegetable garden. You could tell she was really weak.

"*Mrs. B.!*" Anxiously, we gathered around her. At that, we were three steps behind Boom Boom.

I think the players felt as guilty as I did. Here we were, thinking about egg babies, and playoffs, and Cinderella stories, when Mrs. Bolitsky could be really sick. We were selfish jerks!

The coach helped his wife to her feet.

"Are you okay?" asked Alexia without even a hint of reverse volume control.

"I'm fine," she said quickly. "I just felt a little dizzy, that's all."

"Dizzy?" repeated Cal. "Is that bad? That's bad, isn't it?"

"Yeah, what's wrong?" persisted Josh.

She looked at us. I'll bet we were paler than she was, wide-eyed and scared. "Don't you know?"

We stared back at her blankly.

She turned to her husband. "Boom Boom, I thought you were going to tell them."

"I did," shrugged the coach. "The team knows you're whatchamacallit."

Mrs. B. rolled her eyes. "Why can't you speak English for once in your life? I'm not whatchamacallit — I'm *pregnant*! We're going to have a baby!"

"A baby?" echoed Brian.

"We're going to be a father!" roared Cal.

"More like an uncle," Trent amended. He caught a glare from Alexia. "And an aunt," he added hastily.

We went nuts. I mean, the celebration for making the playoffs was *nothing* compared to this. We high-fived Boom Boom and hugged Mrs. B. No wonder she had to miss some of our games! No wonder she was pale and tired! No wonder she wore baggy clothes! All that's *normal* when you're expecting a baby!

Jared got choked up again. "Funny how things work out," he said emotionally. "One life is taken away from us, and now another is coming to fill its place."

"Oh, shut up, Jared," groaned Alexia. "Wendell was an eggshell. This is a *baby*." She turned to me. "And put away that tape recorder, Chipmunk. This is personal. It has nothing to do with your Cinderella story."

"Are you kidding?" I crowed. "We're not Cinderellas anymore. That's kid stuff! With the playoffs *and* a new baby on the way"— I took a deep breath — "the Stars from Mars are the team of destiny!"

Look for Slapshots #4

Cup Crazy

Suddenly, there were oohs and aahs in the auditorium. Onstage, the league officials were hoisting the championship trophy, the gleaming Feldman Cup. It was named after Happer's grandfather, who was the founder of the Waterloo Slapshot League. The current president was also a Feldman — Happer's uncle. And since Happer was on the Penguins, a Feldman was probably going to win the championship this year.

"The league president is holding up the greatest prize in Slapshot hockey," I murmured into my tape recorder.

Happer pinched my neck. "Put your eyes back in your head, Chipmunk. No Martian is ever going to lay an alien finger on that trophy."

Alexia's reverse volume control drifted over her shoulder once more. "Don't make promises you can't keep, bigmouth."

But Happer was smug. "Oh, this one's guaranteed. You'll find out."

Chapter Two

My reporter's sense tingled. What did he mean by that?

But my attention soon shifted to the drama on the stage. The names of the eight playoff teams were placed in the Feldman Cup. Then the draw began.

"The Ferguson Ford Flames will be playing the Powerhouse Gas and Electric Penguins."

Sighs of relief were heard around the room. Everyone knew that a first-round matchup with the Penguins was a sure ticket to an early summer. There were some groans, too, mostly from the Flames.

The Stars drew the Baker's Auto Body Bruins. They beat us pretty badly this year, 6–2. But that was way back in the beginning of the season. The Stars really hadn't had a chance to click at that early point.

I dictated a headline idea into my tape recorder. *"A Shot at Revenge."*

"The Bruins are tough," Trent whispered, "but I think we can take them."

"Let's see how confident you are ten minutes from now," snickered Happer.

Oh, I didn't like the sound of that. Something was up. I could smell it.

After the drawing was finished, we stood around the big chart and tried to map out how we thought the playoffs would go:

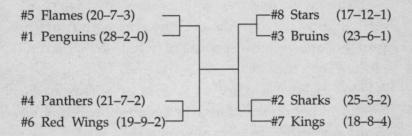

#5 Flames (20–7–3)
#1 Penguins (28–2–0)

#8 Stars   (17–12–1)
#3 Bruins   (23–6–1)

#4 Panthers (21–7–2)
#6 Red Wings (19–9–2)

#2 Sharks   (25–3–2)
#7 Kings   (18–8–4)

"If we get past the Bruins," Josh mused, "then we play the winner of the Sharks against the Kings."

"So long as it's not the Penguins," breathed Jared.

Everyone nodded in agreement. If we had to face the mighty Powerhouse Gas and Electric, it wouldn't be until the final round. That was the way the matchups laid out.

I'll bet we could have stood there all night, figuring the angles while the place emptied out.

Boom Boom grew a little impatient with us. "All right, zip up your whatsits. It's time to get out to the heejazz." *Zip up your coats. It's time to get out to the truck.*

"Hold on there, Bolitsky. I need a word with you and your team."

It was Mr. Feldman. Uh-oh. Happer's uncle was one of those guys who had voted against letting Mars have a team in the Slapshot League. If he had something to say, it was probably bad news.

"Bolitsky," began the league president, "we're all really happy to have Alexia Colwin as your captain. And no one is more proud of what she's accomplished than me."

Don't believe a word of it. The only reason the league let her on the Stars was because the Supreme Court says girls can play anything they want.

Mr. Feldman went on. "But it has come to my attention that it's illegal to have her in the league."

I was so shocked I was tongue-tied. The players were too. But not Boom Boom.

"That's a load of whatchamacallit!" he exclaimed.

"Garbage," Alexia translated quietly.

"I'm just as upset as you are," lied Mr. Feldman. "But the law is the law. It's a Waterloo statute. Have a look." He reached into his breast pocket and produced a photocopy.

We gathered around Boom Boom and stared at the sheet:

Bylaw 14A, paragraph iv: No female personage shall be permitted to hold, or otherwise wield, a length of wood exceeding three feet, with the exceptions of mops, brooms, and butter churns.

Approved April 14, 1887. Yea 4, Nay 1.

"What does this dingus have to do with Alexia?" Boom Boom demanded.

"It doesn't even say anything about hockey," added Trent.

"A hockey stick is a length of wood," Mr. Feldman explained, trying to sound reasonable. "This law states that she can't carry a stick inside city limits." He chuckled. "You certainly wouldn't ask her to play without a stick."

"This is *so* bogus!" howled Jared.

"That stupid law is over a hundred years old!" added Josh.

Mr. Feldman got that superior-adult, snooty look on his face. "The law against murder is even older, and it still counts."

And that's how those rotten Waterloo types

kicked Alexia out of the league. Oh, sure, we fought and hollered and complained. When Boom Boom's excitement level goes up, his English level goes down. He was thingamajigging and doohickeying at top volume.

I couldn't help noticing that Happer was standing behind his uncle, grinning at us with all thirty-two teeth. Now I understood what he'd meant by "Let's see how confident you are ten minutes from now." He'd known about this all along, that jerk!

Mr. Feldman kept saying, "The law is the law." But this wasn't about law. This was another big rip-off against us Marsers! How could the Stars play without Alexia? She was our captain, our second-best player! Her toughness and checking kept the other teams from trying to push us around.

I had one last card, and I played it. "You can't take Alexia away from us!" I argued. "That gives us only nine skaters and a goalie! The league minimum is ten skaters — or do we have to forfeit our playoff spot too?"

"Of course not," said Mr. Feldman. "That would be unfair."

Like he knew anything about fairness!

"The Stars will receive a replacement player," the president went on. "The next boy on the waiting list." He consulted his notebook. "Virgil Knox."

"Fragile!" chorused Jared and Cal in true pain.

We all knew Virgil from Waterloo Elementary School. People called him Fragile because he got a nosebleed every time the wind blew. He was the smallest, shortest, skinniest little dweeb in all of grade six. Eight-year-olds bullied him. In gym class, when choosing up teams, you would try to draft the gerbils out of the science lab before Virgil Knox.

Boom Boom was in such a white-hot rage that he was talking pure doohickeys. Even after Mr. Feldman had gone, the coach was still yelling at the empty space he used to be standing in. I'd never seen the team so mad. Faces flamed red, arms waved, fists clenched. We were all nuts — all except Alexia.

We knew she was upset because she was really quiet. But her expression was as bland as cottage cheese.

"What's everybody surprised about?" she said in a voice so low that we all stopped yelling and strained to hear her. "They always try to mess us up. This is just one more thing."

Josh, her twin, was almost in tears. "Aw, Lex, I'm so sorry! I can't believe they did this to you!"

"How are we going to play without you?" wailed Cal.

"How are we going to play *with* Fragile?" added Jared.

The drive home did nothing to lighten anybody's mood. When we rattled over the bridge into Mars, we were still yelling, and Alexia was still quiet.

About the Author

When he was eleven, Gordon Korman's hockey team had a real Steve Stapleton. "We were last in the standings when he came in. Within a couple of months we were on top of the league and he was the leading scorer. And then people started wondering if maybe this new kid might be too good to be true . . ."

Gordon Korman has written more than twenty books for middle-grade and young adult readers, among them *Liar, Liar, Pants on Fire; The Chicken Doesn't Skate; Why Did the Underwear Cross the Road?; The Toilet Paper Tigers;* and seven books in the popular Bruno and Boots series, all published by Scholastic. He lives with his wife and son in Long Island, New York.